What Dreams

New beginnings take determi........un...

Welcome back to Star Gazer Inn. Alice McIntyre's fresh start after buying the Star Gazer Inn is filling her days, and she's now ready to open with the help of her best friend Lisa's culinary skills and uplifting attitude. And her soon-to-be daughter-in-law Nina by her side, too.

And the magic of her new friend and contractor Seth Roark's tireless attention to detail.

Seth and Alice have both suffered loss, both are starting over, and both are treating this new friendship and attraction they feel toward each other with caution.

Alice's son Dallas is realizing he may not have what it takes to continue riding in the pro rodeo bull riding circuit. He's home at the South Texas McIntyre Ranch after injuring his shoulder and checking out what's going on at his mother's new inn. When he meets a beautiful woman on the beach under unusual circumstances, he has no idea how his life is about to change...

Meanwhile: Riley McIntyre is full speed ahead on getting the new "glamping" venue on the ranch's coastal beachfront property up and going for the ladies who like a little glamor and luxury to their camping experience.

Jackson and Nina are planning their wedding.

Lisa's past is causing problems and with the opening of the inn, Alice needs her to be focused and her culinary skills to be at their best. Can she handle the pressure?

Three women find friendship and courage on the shores of Corpus Christi Bay. Come visit the Star Gazer Inn, with a side trip to the McIntyre Ranch, as Alice finds her way between two worlds.

This new series follows Alice, her sons, and her friends—and new loves—on the South Texas coast with its sparkling topaz water.

You'll want to dip your toes in and stay awhile.

WHAT DREAMS ARE MADE OF

Star Gazer Inn of Corpus Christi Bay, Book Two

DEBRA CLOPTON

What Dreams are Made of
Copyright © 2020 Debra Clopton Parks

CHAPTER ONE

Alice McIntyre stood at the large window of her Star Gazer Inn, her dream—her new dream after having lost the love of her life in a tragic accident two years earlier. Standing there now gazing out at the blue water of Corpus Christi Bay, her thoughts were an odd mixture of both sadness and excitement. Soon, the doors of this inn would open and the first of her guests would arrive, so she should be elated. But she had worked hard the last several months getting it ready for this point, both to open and move forward toward a new future, while letting the sadness of losing her sweet husband, William, settle into a part of her heart. Her heart where he would always be while she pushed herself into a new focus.

She was determined.

And excited. Not just that she was making her

family happy by focusing on her future, but also that she was re-opening the inn where she and William had met. It all just felt right. But there was so much that had happened since she'd made the choice. Starting with hiring her good friend Lisa, who was now the chef for the inn. Her friendship through this had been a blessing. Now, together both of them had a lot riding on this grand opening that would happen in two weeks.

Lisa had had her own problems after a very nasty divorce. Lisa had seemed distracted these last few days and it had Alice a bit worried. Lisa's culinary skills were well-known in the Corpus Christi area as a previously sought-after host for many benefits and for dinner parties that she had held for her ex-husband's clients and friends. He was a very well-known attorney in the area. This made Lisa all the more valuable to Alice for the opening of the inn. People knew her and loved her food.

And yet that wasn't the whole reason she had invited Lisa to be her chef. Mostly it had been because Lisa had been her good friend and they shared a bond of having been through something terrible. They were both fighting to find their footing in this new world that neither of them had asked for. They were determined to move forward together.

Alice had been happy in her long marriage to one of the most well-known cattlemen in the state of Texas and across the United States. She had been well-known at charities and events as the wife of William McIntyre, who was basically a cattle baron. She had enjoyed her life with William and had thoroughly enjoyed being able to be at home and raise her four sons, who were now wonderful young men who ran the ranch and made her proud.

Dallas, her next-to-oldest son, didn't really run the ranch but was a very successful bull riding champion and had made a name for himself and loved what he did. But her other three sons—Jackson, Tucker, and Riley—all worked together to make sure that the McIntyre Cattle Ranch and Enterprises ran smoothly and was a legacy that they wanted to keep up in their dad's memory. She had appreciated that and had loved her life there on the ranch, but she had needed something more after William's tragic drowning in the river accident at the Frio River.

So, she had, on her own, bought this beautiful old inn. She had met William when she had been in her first year of college and working here at the inn. They had fallen in love and met many times at the inn. Now, here at the Star Gazer Inn, she had found something inside her that had died along with William. She had found a new passion, something she could cling to, and she could hear his voice in her head pushing her forward, urging her on, cheering her on. And she stood there, feeling tears in her eyes, knowing that he was happy for her.

Her eyes shifted from the beautiful topaz water of the bay to the new beginnings of a beautiful pavilion that she was having built in the side garden, where she hoped to hold many weddings or other happy events. Looking at the framework, her thoughts shifted to her builder, Seth Roark.

Seth brought more churning to her stomach as she thought about the friendship that she and he had begun. A very unexpected friendship. One she didn't quite understand yet, but one she was cautiously moving forward with. Seth had been through loss himself, having lost his beloved wife to cancer over five years earlier. She was drawn to him because he, too, knew the grief that had stolen her heart. He, too, had had to find his way and he found it not with the Fortune 500 company he had worked for but in working with his hands and building beautiful things. When she had hired him for this job, he had helped her bring the Star Gazer Inn back to its original charm. And recently she had gone on a boat ride with him.

A boat ride...one that had confused her, but she felt optimistic about because they were friends now and had agreed to that. He was in a different stage of his grief and moving forward. She was pushing forward, determined to make William proud of her.

She wasn't certain, though; there was that feeling of hope that she felt every time Seth entered a room. She still wasn't comfortable with the thought that she could ever date again, much less ever fall in love again. After one had known their soulmate, could anything else ever satisfy or replace that? She never believed so. But ever since the boat ride, despite the sensation of hope that she felt—and yes, the attraction that she felt toward Seth—she could only wonder.

To her surprise, her sons had liked that she'd gone on a boat ride with Seth. She hadn't known what to expect but just like they had come through for her when she had told them she was leaving the ranch and opening the inn, they had supported her. They had told her whatever it took for her to move forward, they were behind her and urging her on. They were, after all, their father's sons.

Tears pricked her eyes and she dashed them away. Lisa would be here soon, though she was running late, and she didn't want to have tears in her eyes. Soon after that Seth would be arriving, but at this rate Seth might beat Lisa. Then again, he had told her that he had lumber to pick up before he arrived. Many mornings he met her here and had a cup of coffee with her before he started work. As she stood there, movement caught the corner of her eye and she glanced over to the walkway and saw her neighbor

Nina and her adorable dog, Buttercup.

Nina was smiling and waved as she came up the steps. Alice was happy that someone had arrived to take this sudden melancholy that had set in. She opened the door. "Just the person I needed to see." She gave Nina a hug, then she bent down and caught Buttercup's adorable golden fuzzy face between her hands and rubbed her ears. The pup smiled at her with a big grin.

"She's glad to see you," Nina said.

She looked up at Nina. "And I'm glad to see both of you. There's hot coffee on the counter if you want to get a cup. I'll watch this puppy while you do it."

"Oh, thank you. I'll grab a cup and be right back."

Nina headed inside and Alice gave Buttercup attention. Nina was her neighbor and had a very serious relationship with her oldest son, Jackson. It did Alice's heart good to know that moving here to the Star Gazer Inn had opened the door for Jackson to find the love of his life. And for her to find not only a future daughter-in-law but a really good friend. She stood as Nina came outside with her coffee.

"It's a beautiful morning, isn't it?" Nina's eyes were bright. "We're on our way to visit an art gallery where my paintings are going to be shown in about three weeks. I have to talk to the gallery owner and find out specifically what he's looking for."

6

"Oh, I'm so glad it's not the opening weekend of the inn. But I'm so excited for you and so thankful that you're finally starting to show your artwork again."

When Nina had first moved here she had been hiding her well-known art and keeping a low profile until recently. "Thanks. Me too. But I'm also so excited about the opening of the inn. How are you holding up?"

"I'm getting nervous. It's funny because it's what I want and we're working hard for it, but I have been having some mornings when my stomach was in turmoil."

Nina patted her arm. "It's normal. I can remember my first few gallery showings. I was a wreck. So, you're holding up well. People are going to come out and support you and want to see you succeed. It's going to be a great evening, so don't worry. And for heaven's sake, don't get so nervous you throw up. Thankfully I don't do that anymore."

This was what she had needed. "I'm not that sick, thankfully, but I guess it's just different, you know? I'm truly starting a new stage of my life, moving forward. I guess I'll have my life before William's death and my life after his death. At least in my mind that's how I'm kind of having to catalogue it."

Nina laid a hand on her arm. "I totally understand that. It's not that you love William any less but you can't live in the past, and so you have to take that step forward and you're doing it. And your sons—they all love you and support you. I hope you know that."

"I do. I'm very grateful for them. I was just thinking they are their father's sons, and I hear William in my head saying go, go, go. He's my number-one cheerleader."

"I love that, and Jackson's that for me. I wish I'd met William."

Alice's heart clenched. "I wish you'd met him too. He would have loved you. And he would be so proud that Jackson has found you." Tears welled in Alice's eyes and Nina's too. She reached an arm around Nina's waist, and Nina placed her free arm around Alice's shoulders and they stood there, watching the waves roll in.

* * *

Lisa was running late. She was excited about the opening of the inn and ready to see what the inn could do. She and Alice had worked tirelessly making sure the menu, that would start the night after the opening night party, was all in order. They had a guest list, but it was also an open house where everyone could come to the party, eat the food, and view the place. The restaurant and the hotel officially opened the next day. She was ready.

And she was also nervous.

This was her new start. And she needed it.

Her life had been fairly chaotic since her divorce. The anxiety that she had gone through when Mason had informed her that he was leaving her for a much younger woman, who had given him a son a year earlier, had sent her into a tailspin. *He'd been a daddy for over a year.*

She'd been devastated and furious. In answer, she had hired a good lawyer and had taken everything she could from the divorce, and Mason hadn't fought her on much. Then she had taken her money and her aching heart and whipped spirit, and had gone overseas to get away. She'd gone a little crazy going from place to place, pretending that she was having the time of her life. She went around and cooked with every famous chef she could get a cooking invite from—burying herself in her love of cooking.

In reality, it had been her way of avoiding everyone here in the Corpus Christi area. Her way of avoiding the gossip, the humiliation, the rumors, and the heartache. Finally, though, she'd realized she couldn't hide out forever and she had come home.

No one knew how desolate she was inside, the pain of having had her heart ripped out. Because she had loved her husband. They had been married for six years, and she had believed that they were happy, only to find out that Mason had been living a lie. It was devastating. *How could she have not known?*

That question haunted her.

She had been completely and totally blindsided when he had told her he was leaving her. When she found out that the affair had been going on for nearly two years, it was even more horrifying and humiliating. And she felt stupid.

She felt like an idiot. *How could she have not seen the signs? Had she been so blinded by her love that she had ignored any signs? Had he been such a great actor that he had two lives...* She was still unnerved by the thoughts even now.

And then, over a month ago, he had started texting her, taunting her with pictures of him and his young bride and their son. Lisa had been in shock the first time he had done it. She now had at least twelve pictures, even after she'd told him repeatedly to stop. He hadn't stopped, so she was now trying to ignore him. Yet the man had continued doing it. She never knew when one was coming; they weren't on a regular schedule but instead a surprise. They came unexpectedly, catching her off guard.

And this morning had been one of those mornings. She had gotten a new picture of Tabitha, his bride, and their child smiling into the camera. Did Tabitha even know he was sharing their happy moments with Lisa—his ex-wife?

Again, there was that question: why was he doing this? Just pictures of Tabitha, her happiness, her sexiness—all of it probably designed to make Lisa feel totally deflated and like a loser. He was a scumbag.

Despite that, and to Lisa's horror, this morning she had cried.

And so, she was running late for work. She had had to redo her makeup, splash water all over her face to get rid of her puffy eyes and put on her happy face.

Her happy face that she was determined to make be true.

She *would* be happy. She *would* overcome this, and she *would not* keep feeling so small because her ex-husband was such a sleazeball. He would get his payback; of that she was confident. He would one day be the loser. In fact, Lisa believed that he was already the loser. And maybe that's what all the pictures of Tabitha, him, and the little boy were about—to make him feel as if he wasn't the loser.

As she walked into the inn, Lisa let that thought run through her head. Maybe that was the case. *Maybe he was already feeling like the loser?* No...she doubted it; he was too arrogant to feel that way. But maybe one day.

She breathed deeply, inhaling the scent surrounding her. She would help make a success of this inn. She and Alice would have this dream of theirs become not only the success of Star Gazer Island, the beach town just outside of Corpus Christi, but Corpus Christi and the surrounding area also. Just walking in the door made her spirits lift. Walking down the little hall into the kitchen, she could see out to the gardens and across the gardens, out to the beach and the topaz water. She smiled, this room, her new domain as the chef of the Star Gazer Inn, made her happy.

This was her new beginning. This was her dream. She knew that she was going to find a way to get Mason to leave her alone, because she would not let her ex take her future from her. She just wouldn't do it.

"Alice, where are you?"

"I'm here," Alice said, hurrying in from somewhere down the hall that led into the front area of the inn. "I've been wondering where you were. Nina came by and we had coffee, and I'm looking over some of the ads now. I want your opinion on them."

"Sounds great. I'll be making my final orders today so we make sure we have all of our ingredients in. And the new sous-chef will be coming in tomorrow and we will work together all week, getting prepared. And I'll be having a couple of meetings with the waiters also. So next week is going to be exciting. I just can't believe it's about to happen." Just thinking about it had her pulse pounding.

Alice beamed. "I can't either. And it just looks

great. Seth's going to work all week to finish up the pavilion."

Lisa crossed her arms and leaned against the counter. "Did you go out on the boat with Seth again?" She hoped so, because her friend was smiling a lot lately and maybe he was the reason. Not all guys were like her ex was. Some of them, like Alice's first husband had been and what Seth seemed like, were good guys.

* * *

Alice bit her lip at the question from her friend. "Yes, I did go out on the boat last week with Seth." He had helped renovate the house, and he was a widower, but his wife had passed away a little over five years now while her William had just barely been gone not quite two years. She wasn't sure whether trying to open her heart to someone else was a good idea or a bad idea. All she knew was that when she had agreed to go riding on the boat with Seth, there had been no pressure from him. He had understood where she was and that had been wonderful for her. One of the main things she missed with her William was their companionship. Oh, she missed being his wife, too, and the romantic moments and the intimate moments. But mostly she missed those times they shared when they were just together, having a conversation. So, surprisingly, it had felt good to spend time with Seth.

They had only embraced and that embrace filled her heart and helped fill a longing, a need. Would they go any further than that? Would she ever kiss him? She would think about that when that time came, but for right now she was taking it very slowly. He was her builder and her friend, and it felt good to have him in her corner. He was a lovely man. And her boys liked him. Jackson had spoken for them and told her that whatever she needed to do, they would all support her. She had raised good boys and she knew William would have wanted them to give her that answer.

"He'll be here in a little while to work on the pavilion. He has asked me if I would go out on the boat again with him tomorrow. And I said yes. Does that make you happy?"

Lisa laughed. "It makes me very happy. But the question is, does it make you happy?"

"It actually does. He's just a great guy."

"Yes, he is and from me, saying that after what I've been through? I don't trust any men at the moment, but I have to say he is a great guy. I have watched him closely and I think he's crazy about you. But what I like most about him is he hasn't pressured you. He understands where you're at. And Alice, that's great."

Alice took a deep breath and nodded. "I do too. So, we'll take it slowly. Day to day. Now let's go look at those ads. We are moving forward, and that makes me happy."

"I'm so glad you've chosen to move forward," Lisa said with emotion in her eyes. "It's far better than being down and lost."

Alice sighed. "Yes, it is."

CHAPTER TWO

Dallas McIntyre had arrived in town the day before and strode to the side entrance of his mom's inn with the intention of surprising her. Keeping his injured arm close to his body, he walked around the edge of the large bed-and-breakfast and restaurant. He walked through the back gate and into the garden area of the huge backyard. His mom had the place looking great. He started along the sidewalk to head toward the back porch when he heard a scream coming from the beach.

It wasn't too loud, but he knew what he'd heard. When he heard the scream a second time, he didn't hesitate; he jogged through the garden toward the beach. When he reached the back gate of the inn, he didn't even wait to open it—he just cleared the low fence as if it were a hurdle. His shoulder and upper arm, which was in a painful, weak time right now, screamed with pain. He ignored it and scanned the beach, and saw a woman near the water's edge on her knees, crumpled in the sand. She looked up and screamed again. He raced toward her.

She watched him come with a look of panic in her expression.

He made it to her and went down on his knees. "What's wrong?"

Huge, panic-filled, blue eyes drilled into him. "My baby. My baby is coming."

Baby. He looked down, and only then realized she was pregnant. She was gripping her stomach beneath a pale-yellow gauze shirt that kind of camouflaged how pregnant she was at first glance. "You're having a baby?" He knew the question was stupid because obviously she was, but he wasn't clearly understanding.

She nodded, gasping and clutching her stomach. "Now. I'm having a baby now. I need to get to the hospital."

He was a bull rider. He was not an uncle, a daddy, or a baby doctor. None of the above. He just stared at her.

And then she grimaced, groaned, and clutched her belly. "Help me."

Yeah, help her. Yanking his phone from his

pocket, he dialed his mom's number. "Come on, Mom…answer, answer," he said out loud. He looked at the woman. "My mom lives just right there. At the inn. I'm calling her. We're getting you some help. Just hang on."

His mom answered.

"Mom, I'm out here on the beach. Yes, outside the inn. There's a woman here and she's having a baby. Yes, Mom, out here on the beach—she's having a baby. Call 9-1-1 and get help. I'm fixing to pick her up, and I'm bringing her to the inn. I don't know what's about to happen, but I'm warning you I'm coming, so get ready." And then he hung up.

He rammed the phone back into his pocket and then, as the woman groaned and cried out, he gently picked her up into his arms—his damaged arm cried out too but he ignored it.

Her pants were wet, and he wasn't sure what that was all about, but he knew it had something to do with having a baby. He was panicking. Oh yeah, he was panicking. Past panicking.

She wrapped her arms around his neck and laid her head on his shoulder. "Thank you," she whispered. "I didn't know what I was going to do. He's early. Too early."

Holding her tightly against him, he started toward the inn as fast as he could go. "It's going to be okay.

It's going to be just fine. My mom's making a phone call. We're going to put you there at the inn—you'll be comfortable, and she'll know what to do. So just rest easy."

She nodded against his neck and then groaned, and he felt her stomach against his belly tighten, really tighten. And he wanted to run. Instead, he walked as fast as he could toward the back entrance of the Star Gazer Inn, never so happy to see a back glass door open in all of his life.

His mom raced down the steps and came to meet him. "Dallas, come on, bring her in here. Oh, my goodness."

His mom wasn't one to panic, thank goodness, but her words told him this was not a normal circumstance. Something he already knew. She raced back up the steps to hold the door open as he moved inside.

"Take her into the first bedroom down the front hall."

He moved in that direction, following her extended arm, and she fell into place behind him. He was relieved to see Lisa, a good friend and chef, laying towels on the bed.

She smiled at him. "Come on in, Dallas. Lay her here. We're going to take care of her until the ambulance gets here."

He could only hope so.

"They won't be long," his mother added. "So hang in there, darlin'. You and the baby are going to be fine."

Dallas prayed his mom and Lisa were right.

* * *

Lorna Jordan fought tears as pain ripped through her. She clung to the man's neck, who had raced across the sand to her rescue. She didn't know how she could ever repay him for what he was doing for her. Her baby was two weeks earlier than expected. She would have never come to walk on the beach if she had thought she was going to go into labor.

Her poor baby boy. Surely he would be okay.

The first woman smiled. "Come on, darling, you have to let go of Dallas so we can lay you on the bed here. The ambulances are on their way. Lisa and I— I'm Alice—we're going to help you out. And I might not have ever delivered a baby, but I've helped deliver a lot of cows in my day, and so has Dallas. It is a little bit similar, so if we have to, we can take care of you. Now come on."

She looked into the man's face. *Dallas.* He had kind eyes and they were full of concern. She blinked hard because just looking at him made the tears want to flow harder, but she would not cry. "Thank you," she whispered and then she let go of his neck.

"I'm just glad I was there. But I can tell you that I might have delivered some calves, but that's as far as my knowledge goes. However, my mama here, she's had a few babies herself. I'm going to turn you over to her. However, if they need me for anything, they know I'm right here, but I'm going to step out and let them take care of you." He stepped back.

His mother took his place and smiled kindly at her. "Everything's going to be just fine. I'm just thankful that Dallas found you. Are you early?"

Lorna nodded. "Two weeks. I didn't think he was going to come early. Is two weeks too early? Too dangerous?"

"No, darling, two weeks is just fine for your baby. Ahead or after is fine, so you're going to be okay. He's just eager to get here. All my boys were eager to get here. They all tried to rush me. So, you just hang in there. As a matter of fact, Dallas there was three weeks early and look what a strong, big man he turned out to be. And he rides bulls, so there's nothing wrong with him. Maybe a little dense in the head to pick riding bulls as a full-time job, but he's good at it, so I guess he knew what he was doing. Now the ambulance will be here in a minute but let's talk about how far apart your pains are coming."

"I'm not sure."

Alice looked at her friend. "Lisa, maybe you need to put a pot of water on the stove and get it to boiling just in case we need to sterilize something before the ambulance gets here. And go ahead and bring me some soft towels."

"I'll do it. Yeah, young lady, you're in good hands with my friend Alice. She'll take good care of you."

Alice was kind-looking, and there was something in her eyes, a determination that calmed Lorna. She nodded. "I believe you. I'm just thankful I'm not out there alone on that beach. It was pretty deserted this morning."

Alice patted her arm. "God didn't have a plan for you to be having this baby out there all by your lonesome. So there you go…you've got that on your side right now."

A pain grabbed hold of her again. She yelped, cupped her stomach, and bent forward as the need to push slammed into her. "I think I need to push," she gasped.

"No." Alice waved Lisa to go. "Just hold on. Try to breathe. Come on, try to breathe and try to relax. Just try to give it a few more minutes. I think I hear the ambulance in the distance." She moved to a new position. "I'm going to take a look and see what you look like and make sure the baby isn't already showing up."

"Mom, I'll wait to let the emergency team in." Dallas left the room.

Lorna was thankful when seconds later she heard the sirens. She breathed in and out as Alice instructed. And it seemed to calm her a little bit and helped the pains not be so hard. She relaxed a little more as the need to push lessened. *If she could just hang on.*

"Okay, you're relaxed, so if we can get them in here before you feel the need to push again, things will be just fine and you won't have to worry about having your baby delivered by me."

"Thank you, Alice."

"You're welcome. What is your name?"

She inhaled and her hand went back to her stomach, but she was able to speak. "Lorna."

"It is so very nice to meet you, Lorna." Alice patted her hand again just as the door opened.

Dallas came into the room and Lorna breathed a sigh of relief as she met his gaze, and he nodded at her. Then she saw he was leading the way for two paramedics. She tried to smile but the pain hit her, and she couldn't get a smile out to let him know how much she appreciated him.

Because that was her problem: she had no one. She had thought she would take a walk on the beach and try to figure out her life. Try to figure out what her next step was with a baby she had not planned but knew she wanted to raise. But no answer came. Instead, this happened. It was almost as if God was telling her nothing in her life was going to get any easier. And she believed it.

But as Dallas backed out of the room, her eyes held his until he gave her a nod and returned to the hallway. He had rescued her and her baby, and she was so very grateful.

* * *

Dallas was pacing the kitchen when his mom entered. "Is she going to be okay?"

"Yes. She looked really worn out," Lisa added.

"She's going to be fine. Those paramedics are going to take care of her but she's going to have that baby right now in there. I'm thankful they got here when they did. Goodness, I'm so glad you found her. How did you find her?"

"I was coming to see you, and I had just come into the garden when I heard a scream. I ran there onto the sand and she was out there by the water, with nobody around. Nobody would have heard her calling if I hadn't been outside." He rammed his hand through his hair. "She would have had that baby alone on the beach. It's a terrible thought."

His mom placed a hand on his arm and squeezed.

"She didn't because God put you in the right place at the right time."

He was grateful he had been there. "I'm glad you and Lisa were home. I don't know what I'd be doing if it had just been me trying to deliver that baby right now."

"Darlin'," his mom said. "You've delivered a lot of livestock, so you would have managed."

Lisa came over and gave him a hug and looked up at him. "Dallas, your mom is right. You've delivered a lot of calves, so you are no stranger to stress. If you can get on the back of a bull, all calm, cool, and collected, you would have delivered that baby with flying colors, I'm confident."

"I agree with Lisa. You could have done it. You are just feeling jittery right now because it's an unknown thing to you."

He sighed. "Well, I'm glad y'all have confidence in me, but I still say that poor woman would have been in trouble if that baby's birth were in my hands."

His mom patted his shoulder. "You would have come through."

He took a deep breath. He had almost had to deliver a baby but thank goodness, he hadn't had to.

CHAPTER THREE

Seth Roark turned onto Main Street and headed toward the end of the small island. He was running late to get to work this morning at the Star Gazer Inn, and he was ready to see Alice. But he had to stop and pick up the lumber he needed and some other supplies for the pavilion he was building in the garden at the inn.

After he had lost his beloved wife to cancer almost six years ago, it took so much out of him. Losing her was like losing half of himself, and he hadn't felt as though he fit in anywhere. It took a long time for him to find joy again. Although he had been determined to move forward like his wife would have wanted, that didn't include finding another spouse. He just wasn't ready to think about that and was not sure he ever would be. Losing Jen had knocked the life right out of him. Thankfully, he had found solace in his boat. He took his boat out often and alone, fishing sometimes and other times just enjoying the day. Sometimes just sitting out there on the water, letting the waves rock the boat as he enjoyed the quietness.

During her illness, he'd been on leave from his executive job. But after Jen died, he didn't go back. He took an early retirement and then, he'd started his renovating business. He'd been in business nearly five years when he took the job of renovating the inn. Where he met Alice McIntyre, and something inside him had cracked. He'd been attracted to her instantly. Something that hadn't happened since Jen died.

Alice was a more recent widow and he respected her very much with how she was trying to push herself forward and start fresh, start a new life. She was clearly at a crossroads and not ready to date. He understood where she was at because he'd been there too—until meeting her.

He liked that she and her husband had had such a wonderful marriage, like he had had with Jen. He had been startled how he had come to feel about her during the weeks that he renovated the inn. He was being very careful to move slowly and had no intentions of rushing her. The last thing he ever wanted to do was hurt her, and they would only move forward if and when she was ready.

When she had agreed to go on his boat with him, he had been on cloud nine and stayed there ever since. They'd had a great time, as friends, but had hugged while on the boat as he'd comforted her. He'd felt that she had feelings for him and the best thing he could do was not to rush her.

He had begun wishing that he could hold her more often than the few times he'd comforted her. He pushed the thoughts out of his mind, knowing that he was rushing things and it would only make him frustrated to let himself look at a future with Alice right now. And yet, he knew he wanted more between them.

He had been thrilled that she agreed to go on the boat with him again this weekend. It had had him whistling every morning, like now.

Ambulance lights flashing in the driveway of the inn stopped his whistling. His heart plummeted, hit rock bottom, and then bounced back into his throat. *Was something wrong with Alice?*

He was swept back to the many times the ambulances were called for Jen. He yanked the steering wheel and pulled the truck at an awkward angle in front of the inn. Jumping out of the vehicle, he raced up the drive, up the steps, and through the open door. He ran through the hallway and nearly collapsed when he spotted Alice across the room, talking with

Dallas and Lisa. Her eyes met his, and he knew he had already fallen for Alice McIntyre, totally and completely.

Swallowing hard, he rushed toward her and wrapped his arms around her. "Alice, what is happening? I thought something may have happened to you." He released her, fighting hard not to hang on to her. He had to get hold of himself.

"It's okay. We've had some excitement. We're having a baby in the next room. Dallas rescued a woman in labor from the beach. And the paramedics are with her right now. I'm very relieved they made it in time, because for a moment there, I thought I was going to have to deliver the baby." She smiled at him and touched his arm.

Relief flooded through him. He forced his expression to relax and he smiled. "Well, all I can say is I'm glad I was late getting here this morning, and that I wasn't in the garden, and that I wasn't the one who had to find the woman on the beach. How did you find her out there?"

Dallas inhaled. "I was coming to visit Mom and entered the backyard and heard a scream. I raced to the beach and found her and got her here to Mom and Lisa to help deliver her baby."

"Believe me," Alice said. "I would have done what I had to do but it was a relief to see the EMTs walk through those doors like heroes."

He couldn't help himself; he placed his hand over hers and squeezed. "Then I'm glad they showed up so you didn't have to go through that stressful situation."

In that moment, they heard a baby cry. They all turned toward the door as the baby cried again.

"Is that normal, Mom?" Dallas asked.

"That's normal." She smiled at him. "That's a good thing when the baby cries. Dallas, I'm so thankful you found her."

Dallas nodded. "Oh, no more than I am. Matter of fact, I hope this never happens again but I'm going to watch a few YouTube videos on how to deliver a baby in an emergency situation. Just in case this ever happens again."

They all smiled at him, and then the door opened, and the paramedics came out, pulling the stretcher.

* * *

The ambulance left and Dallas followed them. Alice looked at the group standing with her in the driveway. "Well, that was an experience for us, and for Lorna. I don't know if we should go to the hospital, or let Dallas be there and fill us in? She's got to be worn out."

Seth placed a hand on her shoulder and squeezed. "You've been amazing in helping her just in the short time until the ambulance arrived, from what I can see. Looks to me like you can do whatever you want to, so if you want to go to the hospital, I'll take you. You too, Lisa."

"No." Lisa waved her hands. "I don't have long before the hotel opens, so I want to keep tweaking my menu. Come by in a little while and have a taste of some of my opening night desserts."

"And me…" Alice crossed her arms and looked at him with uncertainty. "I don't know what I should do. But I think maybe we could go now."

He grinned. "Yes, I kind of figured that would be the plan. Come on, let's go. Do you have what you need?"

"I have to grab my purse and I'll be ready." She smiled at him and headed inside.

He opened the door of the truck when Alice came back out with her purse. He would do anything for this woman. Watching her be delighted about having been a part of this birth was beautiful. She was coming back into her old self, and that was good for everybody. Which, as far as he knew, considering he had begun working for her a few months ago, she had been working in that direction from day one. She climbed

31

into the seat and then smiled at him and his entire inner self smiled back.

"Thank you for taking me. I probably won't stay long but we'll just be able to check in on her and see if she needs anything. I mean, she was out there by herself. I didn't see a phone or anything." She looked at him. "You know, her vehicle might be around here."

"You're right. While we're driving, see if you see any unusual vehicles parked along the road or in the beach parking lot up there. Although it's quiet out there this morning, in this area there might be so many you can't see an unknown vehicle."

"I'll keep my eyes out for one anyway."

He closed the door, and then got in on his side. Within seconds, they were driving down the street. She pointed out a couple of vehicles that normally were not there. If they got to talk to her, they could ask what vehicle she drove.

"I'm glad that Dallas was out there," Seth said. "Did he just get back to town?"

"Yes. And I'm glad he's back. His shoulder and arm is having a major problem, and he had to stop competing for a while. He actually may need to retire. He loves the rodeo, but his shoulder is bad."

"Wow. And he carried her in from the beach?"

"Yes. I'm not sure how."

"Determination. And maybe God has a plan."

She cocked her head and looked at him. "I was thinking the same thing. Did you see how determined he was to go to the hospital?"

"Yes, I did. Interesting." He glanced back at her, wondering what she was thinking.

"I'm hoping it is a positive experience for him. For both of them."

Seth hoped so too.

CHAPTER FOUR

Alice hugged Dallas the moment she saw him in the waiting room. "Have you heard anything about Lorna?"

"Lorna?"

"Yes, did you not know her name?"

He shook his head. "No. But thanks. They're getting her in a room now. And she's doing good. I'm glad I found her on the beach."

"You were meant to be there." She nodded at him because it was true.

"I figure I'll go in and check on her and see if there is anything she needs me to do." His expression was serious. "I don't know if she has anyone around."

"That sounds like a good plan then. You can let us know how she is and if she needs anything."

"Well, Mom, I'm sure you can go in too. I mean, it's not like I know her."

She glanced at Seth, and he raised an eyebrow. Her mind whirled and she looked back at her son. "I think that it might be hard enough on her without a bunch of strangers going in there, so I just wanted to come by and tell you we are here for you, and if she needs anything to call us and we'll get it. Believe me, I want to see this baby and meet Lorna again, but I don't feel like now is the time. I'm going to have this man right here take me back to the inn so we can get started on our final project. But seriously, if she needs *anything,* let me know."

Dallas looked a little mystified by her words but nodded. "I will, Mom, and I'm sure this has been a pretty tremendous day for her, so you might be right— less action this evening could be the best thing."

When she and Seth reached the parking lot again, she paused. "I don't know what I'm doing, but that felt right. He found her, he rescued her, and now I'll let him go from here. I'm sure maybe tomorrow or the next day we'll meet her. Anyway, do I sound like a crazy person?"

Seth reached for her hand. "You sound like someone who wants something good for her son."

"I do. But I don't know anything about her, not even if she's already married. But at least he's helping.

Helping someone is always beneficial to someone who is down. Thanks for being there for me."

"Always," he said, and squeezed her hand gently.

She was actually very thrilled at Seth's reaction to her craziness. He didn't think she had lost her mind. He seemed to think she was acting like a mom who cared and he agreed. Seth was a great guy. And looking at him now just increased her like for him. He had been so good to her through the remodeling of her bed-and-breakfast and the making of the restaurant into a large and great place. And now he was going to make her a beautiful pavilion where people could get married if they wanted to. Or have anniversary presentations or renew their vows. "So, are you ready to work in the garden today?"

He grinned at her as he opened the truck's door. "Yes, I am. I'm ready. Are you ready to make sure I do it like you want?"

Alice chuckled. "Yes, I am. I surely am. I can't wait to see another masterpiece you create." And she meant it.

* * *

Lorna's heart swelled with love as she glanced at the beautiful baby boy in her arms. She still couldn't believe she had made it through the morning and been helped so much in order for her baby to get here. She heard the door of her room push open and glanced up with anticipation. Dallas poked his head into the room and an intense feeling of gratitude filled her.

She smiled as she met his gaze. "Hello, Dallas. Please come in."

"Okay," he said quietly and eased into the room, then closed the door behind him. He walked within six feet of the bed and stopped. "How's it going?"

"Because of you, it's going well. And Dallas, my name is Lorna Jordon, and I am so grateful to you. Please come over here so you can see him better." She waved him over and switched the baby to the opposite arm so he would be facing Dallas. "Meet Landon. He's named after my father, who died when I was seven. He was a very nice man." She meant every word about her dad and had been thrilled to name a child after him.

"It's nice to meet you, Lorna. He's handsome. Ah, look—he's grinning at you." He looked at her. "And I'm sorry you lost your dad. I lost mine two years ago, so I was blessed to have him around a longer time, but at least you had your dad long enough to get to know him a little bit and have good memories."

Their gazes locked and she felt an undeniable connection with Dallas.

"Thank you." She looked down at Landon. "I

think he's adorable. And I'm grateful to have him. I want to thank you for hearing my voice and rushing to save my sweet baby. If you hadn't shown up, I don't know what would have happened."

He bit his lip. *The man was so handsome when he bit his lip.* He was adorable. She really had a problem. Most likely because she had just given birth to this precious baby and her emotions were churning.

"You're very welcome," he said after a second. "I'm just glad that I was there to do it."

They stared at each other. And she was at a loss for words. Then her baby suddenly made a noise and they both looked down at him. He had a smile on his face. And he grinned bigger as they looked on.

"Wow, he's happy." Dallas chuckled.

She was too. "Yes, but you know they tell me that means he needs to go to the bathroom or something, but I'm going to take it as he's happy because I certainly am."

"So, I'm going to be a little bit nosy here," he said. "Do you have everything you need at your house or your apartment? Do you have some family I could call? If not, then I can get it for you."

Anything she needed? She ignored the tugging of her heart. "Actually, I have no family. And I don't know anyone here, since I've only been here for a couple of weeks. Is there any way you can take me home when they release me? I do have a house."

Yes, she had a house—under very odd circumstances.

"Yes. I'll do whatever you need. So, no worries about that, okay?"

Her heart raced, and her relief surged, because she had been worried, she would have to have a taxi come to pick her up. This was so much better.

CHAPTER FIVE

Nina Hanson drove up the drive of the McIntyre Ranch. It never ceased to freak her out a little bit to realize that she was about to be part of this gigantic ranch as soon as she and Jackson were married. It was a miracle to her that she had come to this tiny little island of Star Gazer to get away from a stalker and in the process met Jackson and his mom and Lisa and all the people of Star Gazer and the Star Gazer Inn. It had taken three years of living in seclusion at the end of the little island with the vacant inn as her only neighbor. And then Alice McIntyre bought the inn and moved in, and her life had changed upon meeting Jackson.

Of course, her life would have changed just from meeting his wonderful mom and her friend Lisa, who had both become some of her closest friends. But Jackson was the topping on the cupcake. He was amazing. And it didn't matter whether he came from this gigantic ranch or a little cabin in the middle of nowhere; she couldn't wait to become his wife.

When he stepped out of the big barn and waved, her heart thundered in her chest and she waved back, then parked the car. Smiling, he strode over, opened her door and took her hand to help her out of the vehicle. Once out, he immediately swept her into his arms, lowered his head, and kissed her deeply.

Instantly, her knees weakened.

"I am glad you're here. I missed you." He lifted his head and winked at her. "I always miss you. You know that, right?"

She loved him so much. "I do, and I feel the same way. I can't wait until we figure out a good date for this wedding. Because I'm so ready."

"Well, we're going to look at that calendar more closely and we're going to get it figured out because I'm tired of this. I'd marry you at the justice of the peace, but I know you want and deserve more than that."

"I would marry you at the justice of the peace, but you know good and well we want friends and family there."

"Yes, we do. And I want you to have the beautiful wedding that you deserve."

"I just want you."

"And now you're just getting sappy. Which I love." He chuckled and kissed her again, pulling her close and setting every nerve in her body dancing.

They pulled away and walked toward the barn. She was happy. "So did the babies come?"

"Yes, they did. You're about to see two of the most beautiful colts you've ever seen. It's crazy that they came last night."

"At the same time is unbelievable. But you said you had a feeling they were going to come really close together."

"Yeah, I just had a feeling when I called the vet. When he got here, he felt the same way and spent most of the night out here getting these two foals into the world. One was not an easy birth but thankfully is okay. He and I were both tired at three in the morning when he got to head home."

"Oh, did you get to sleep? I didn't have to come out this morning—you could have rested."

"I got some rest. Besides, I'm glad to see you. I hope your trip to Dallas was good. I wish I had been able to drive you down."

"The art gallery was beautiful, and the show there next month will be good, I think." She'd had to go down and check out the spot and was pleased. This weekend was her first show in a long time, and it was here in town. She was looking forward to it. "I would have loved you driving me down, but your business is important, too, and you needed to be here. Those colts are part of your championship bloodlines and mean a lot to the ranch."

"True. But you mean more to me than any of this."

She looked up at him, so touched by his declaration. "I believe you. But that doesn't mean you have to be irresponsible and not be here for something important like this. Oh, my goodness." She spotted the colts and their mothers in stalls beside each other. "Beautiful."

The colts were walking around in their stalls, and they weren't completely wobbly as she'd thought they would be. They were small-bodied and long-legged; one was the beautiful color of buff suede and one was a pale brown. They were gorgeous. She could have watched them moving around all day.

She looked at Jackson. "I don't think I could ever get tired of seeing something as stunning as this."

His lips spread into a smile of agreement. "Same here. They're amazing, aren't they? Only thing better is a new human baby being born. Then again, I could look at you all day long."

She smiled. "Speaking of which, once we get this date on our marriage settled, then we'll know sooner when we can have our own beautiful babies."

He pulled her into his arms again and kissed her forehead. "I agree. So we're going to go in my office right now and we're going to figure it out. If I have to cancel something, I will."

They had been trying to work around all of his commitments. He had a busy schedule with meetings, some around the world. The running of the huge McIntyre Ranch empire had fallen on all of his brothers after losing their dad, but Jackson was the lead. He was the one who had stepped to to fill what his dad had done and that put a lot on his shoulders. The last thing she had wanted to do was put more on his shoulders. And now she was booking art shows, so they had a fairly complicated schedule to weed through.

"I'm all for a quick marriage at the justice of the peace."

"No, I've told you before—I want to give you the wedding you deserve."

Getting the wedding set was really bothering him now, and she knew they were going to have to set a date just for his peace of mind. But she hadn't been kidding when she said that she would get married at the justice of the peace. She definitely would have an intimate service with just his family there and it would have been lovely. But that wouldn't be fair to friends of his family who loved his mother and dad and wanted to see their oldest son happy. Thus, she let him lead her inside and hoped they could come up with a date that everyone could make.

CHAPTER SIX

"Morning, everyone," Riley said as he met his brothers in the kitchen for coffee before they started their day.

"Morning." Tucker took a sip of coffee. "Did you hear what Dallas did yesterday?"

He looked at Dallas. "I was gone most of the day. What happened?"

"He played rescue man," Jackson said as he poured himself a cup of coffee.

"Really? What'd you do?" Riley knew his rodeo brother had come home because his shoulder was messed up and he noticed the icepack on it now.

"I went to see Mom and was entering through the backyard when I heard a desperate call from the beach. I ran out there and found Lorna. She was in labor. I got her back to Mom's and thank goodness, Mom took over. We have a really special mom and she was able to calm Lorna, giving the ambulance time to show up."

"Wow. Is the baby okay?"

"Yeah, I'm about to head back up there to the hospital and I'm going to drive her home if they decide to let her go today. If not, then I'll do it tomorrow."

"Glad it wasn't me." Tucker hitched his brow. "But we all know you can accomplish anything, Dallas."

Everyone agreed. Dallas was one who could usually handle whatever he set his mind to. But with his shoulder, things were slowing down.

Riley felt for him because he was pretty sure his shoulder was going to cost Dallas the sport he loved. Riley nodded at his shoulder. "How's that doing? Did you have to carry her?"

"Yeah, he did," Tucker said. "He won't say it, but he's in a lot of pain."

"I'll make it. The icepack and the ibuprofen painkiller is going to help." Dallas looked at the ice. "I've had to make this work during a ride."

Riley knew his brother was fighting a life-changing fight. "Okay, I hope you're right. Why doesn't she have someone to take her home?"

"I don't think she has anyone here. I don't know everything, but she seems to have just moved into town."

"I find that very interesting," Jackson said. "But she was very lucky you rescued her."

"I'm just glad I heard her." Dallas looked grateful. "Okay, I'm heading out. Y'all have a good day."

"You have a good day and let us know if we can do anything for her," Riley said.

"Yeah," Jackson agreed. "After you get a look at her place, let us know if she needs anything."

"Sure thing. Thanks."

Tucker looked very serious. "She's very lucky you were there. I'm glad you were."

"Me too." Dallas removed his icepack then headed out the door.

Riley watched him go, as did they all. "Well, fellas, this is interesting."

"You think?" Jackson said. "Dallas arrived with no plans and this happened almost immediately. It'll give him something to distract him from the change that is happening in his professional life."

They all agreed.

Riley knew his brother was going to have a hard, hard time giving up what he loved. He, on the other hand, had never had a job he loved like that. But he'd recently had a job spark his interest. "Okay, so I've got to go. I just came in to say bye for the weekend," Riley said. "I have a ladies' weekend to see to for tomorrow."

His brothers all laughed and chuckled.

"Hey, don't judge."

Tucker grinned. "Are you going to spy?"

"No, I'm going to be the maintenance man." He set his cup in the sink and headed for the door. He had been researching women's camps for a bit now, ever since he'd met a beautiful woman at the gas station, pulling a very interesting small camper. He'd cleaned her windows for her and been interested but she didn't give him her name. But as he watched her driving away, he'd realized he had a perfect spot on the ranch's beach area that could be a camping spot. Not just a regular camping spot but a glamor spot like these women were using for weekend trips. A camping area that had special things going on, like massages, facials, and other things—things he hoped to see this weekend.

He was checking out a camp, having seen their maintenance man had gotten sick and they had an opening. He'd called immediately and now had an interesting weekend planned.

He was hoping that maybe the woman from the gas station might be there. But who knew. That might be a long shot.

* * *

It had turned out to be a great September day as Dallas pulled the truck into the parking area of a very nice ranch and stopped. He was in shock when he had started down the drive, taking Lorna home. For some reason, a ranch was the last place he'd imagined she lived.

He looked over at her. "This is nice." His family ranch was on the opposite side of town but not terribly far away.

She looked odd as she glanced around. "Yes, it is. I've been here for about two weeks and I'm still getting used to it. I'll explain later. We need to get the baby inside and into bed. Then hopefully I'll have the energy to explain the ranch."

"Sounds like a plan." He got out, then opened the back door and unlatched the baby carrier that was locked into the seat belt and worked as a carrier and a car seat.

Lorna strode slowly up the sidewalk and went to a side door that had a patio outside it. He noticed the overgrown grass everywhere as he followed. The place was nice but needed some attention.

She reached the door and opened it. "Come on in."

He walked past her, then waited as she came in and then moved past him. She looked tired and he wanted to get her seated and resting. He walked into the kitchen area and was impressed by the room. It was masculine, with dark wood, but nice.

She kept walking past the kitchen bar through to

the living room, which was also impressive. She continued going and turned a corner into a hallway and entered into the second room. He followed her into the baby's room. It was not decorated like some baby's rooms that he had seen, but it did have a cute white baby bed, blue covers, and a couple of baby animals. And there was a blue-and-white checked rocker.

"Nice room." He set the baby carrier in the chair and she unbuckled the baby, then picked him up. Landon smiled in his sleep. Dallas didn't care what they said about smiling babies and passing air or whatever they thought it was; this baby really smiled. At least, it seemed that way to him.

Lorna smiled too and laid Landon in the crib, then quickly checked his diaper and smiled when it was still clean. She pulled a thin blanket up over his little hips. She sighed, looking at her baby, and Dallas watched her. Her expression was clearly one of love, and it was very easy to see.

She looked over at him, then started toward the door. "I better go in the living room and sit down. If you'd like something to drink, there's water and orange juice in the refrigerator."

"No, thank you, I'm fine. You look really tired. Come on, let's get you in a seat."

They walked back into the living room. A chair with an ottoman and a blanket was in a position where the occupier would have a living room view and a kitchen view, though it was at the far end from the kitchen. She immediately walked to it and sank into the seat, then took the blanket and laid it over herself as she put her feet on the ottoman.

She looked up at him. "I have to just get my energy back."

"Yes, and you will. But, in the meantime, do you have anybody to come out here and help you?"

She closed her eyes and leaned her head onto the back of the chair. "No, I'm afraid I don't. I have to get used to this."

This was so odd. He glanced around the room. There was nothing in this room that looked like her. It was as if a cowboy had lived here and lived here alone. He saw a picture on the wall, and strode over to it. He saw that it was of a roper who he'd known slightly, but at the moment his brain was too confused to come up with his name.

"I'm going to get you some water." He headed to the kitchen.

"That picture is of Lewis Franks. He's Landon's father. He had a fast-acting cancer and he died about three months ago. I don't usually have a relationship like that. I had dated him three times when he came to Houston one week. I truly don't normally do that, and on that night, I knew I'd messed up. I wasn't drawn to him like I should have been if I was going to get that personal. And he shut himself into the bathroom for a while afterward. I could tell he was just as sorry about what we'd done as I was. He left quickly and was flying home the next day. I heard from him once a few days later when he called to tell me he was ill, had been ill for a few months, and wouldn't be back to Houston again. I felt bad for him but was fine that I wouldn't see him again. And then, about a week later, I started feeling sick in the mornings. When I finally took a test and saw I was pregnant, it was hard to adjust."

He crossed the room and held the glass of water out to her. "I'm sure it was. Here, drink some of this."

She looked at her hands and he felt for her. She must have been greatly shocked.

"Thank you." She met his gaze with eyes full of emotion. "Then I had to call him again. And he was shocked almost more than I was. He was also weak—I could hear it in his voice. He was still sick. He asked me questions and then, with a cracking voice, he told me he was dying before the birth of the baby but that he would make sure we were taken care of. I couldn't believe it, and I felt so sorry for him. He had been skinny when I went out with him, but dying was just unbelievable. And I didn't know what he meant about taking care of us. I assumed he might be leaving me a little money, but I wasn't sure. I didn't hear from him again all during the first seven months. Then he passed away a little over a month ago and I got a call from his lawyer to come here for the reading of the will." She took a breath, then a drink of water.

"This sounds really hard for you."

"Yes. When I got here to this house, we came here in the living room, and I was the only person here with the lawyer. I almost passed out. My apartment in Houston was very small and my job wasn't going to be great for me as a single mom, trying to work and take care of a baby at the same time. I was kind of in a fix. But when the lawyer read the will and I learned I was inheriting the ranch, and income and other things, I was in shock. It wasn't just a big ranch—it was money to live on. It was inherited property owned by him. And then there are the cattle and horses. I'm not a huge ranch person, so I'm a little confused right now."

Dallas was totally in shock. What a story. This woman had a complicated situation but goodness, to have inherited this ranch with the horses and the cows and a place for her baby was a blessing to her. He was going to ask his brothers what they knew about Lewis Franks. He was older than Dallas, so obviously, from what he could figure, guessing Lorna's age to be around twenty-nine, Lewis had been several years older than her.

"That story is amazing. So you own this place and you have an income coming in."

"Yes. I have to get used to everything, but I don't have any financial worries or home worries. I just have to adjust to it."

"Well, that is a blessing," he said. She looked exhausted and needed to pause talking for a while. "I'm going to go in your kitchen and make some lunch. You sit there and rest, and we'll get you fed and then check the baby again. How does that sound?"

Her eyes were closed and she nodded. "Thank you. Thank you very much."

"I'm glad to be here helping you." And he was.

Dallas went to the kitchen, his thoughts going over everything he had just learned. This girl needed help. It was completely obvious. He opened the refrigerator and thankfully saw an unopened container of turkey lunchmeat. He pulled it out, along with a jar of mayonnaise. He also grabbed the orange juice because he assumed she probably needed some vitamins. He glanced in the living room and she looked as if she were sleeping. *She was tired and alone.* His brain whirled with worry for her.

He set the sandwich stuff on the counter and then grabbed the loaf of bread he had seen at the end of the counter. He opened the cabinets until he found the plates and pulled out two. He quickly made two sandwiches and put them each onto a plate. It needed more, so he went into the pantry and grabbed a half-full bag of plain potato chips. She needed supplies. There was not much in here. He would have to offer to go to the store for her.

After he had some chips on their plates, he strode back into the living room and set the plate on the table beside her chair. He set the glass of orange juice next to it. Then he went back in and grabbed his and came back. She was still lying with her eyes closed.

His heart raced as he reached out and touched her hand. "Lorna, your lunch is here."

She opened her blurry eyes and met his, and smiled. When she smiled, his heart did funny things.

"Thank you. Maybe that will give me energy." She picked up half of the sandwich, since he had sliced them in half, and took a bite.

He took a bite also and gave her time to get some food in her stomach. She was almost finished with the first half of the sandwich when he knew what he needed to do.

"So here's what I'm thinking. I have come back home recently because my shoulder and upper arm is really messed up. Not that it's ruined for life, but it could be if I continued with what I'm doing. I may have to have surgery on it. I know a lot of guys who keep on bull riding after they have surgery, then have to have another surgery. Anyway, I'm here for now to get well as I can before making any decision about my next move. They don't need me at the ranch with my one arm, so I'm going to be your helper. If you don't mind.

"I can look out your window and see that you need your yard mowed. You have horses and cows that may need some care. I can see them out there in the pasture, and I'm hoping there's none inside the barn because that means they haven't been fed in two days, unless he has someone coming by. But anyway, just in case there is no one, I can take care of all that for you and help you here around the house and with the baby while you need me to. So don't worry, I'll go out there and check everything out and feed the animals and then check out the lawn mower. If I don't get to start it today, I will begin in the morning."

A tear ran down her face. "Are you sure? I don't really know what else to do. The guy who was feeding them had accepted another job, the lawyer told me. Thank goodness there is grass out there so they've been able to eat it, and there is water. But they probably need things. I know nothing about cows or horses."

He was in, and oddly, he was thrilled. "I'll take

care of them. And you don't have to pay me anything. This is a volunteer offer."

"But I can pay you."

"No. I'm doing this as a friend."

She looked away and he sent a quick prayer up of thankfulness that he had been able to rescue her off the beach when she was in such need, and now he would be able to help her more.

CHAPTER SEVEN

Alice stared at the gazebo and was filled with great joy. Seth had hit it perfectly. "It's looking so very amazing."

"I'm glad it's looking like you want." Seth stood near the top of the ladder as he finished adding a piece of wood on the corner.

"I'm amazed at how fast you got this up."

"Three days is not bad. And we'll get the shingles on the roof tomorrow."

She still couldn't believe how fast he was. "Well, it's almost time for you to get off. Do you want to come have a cup of coffee or maybe a dessert?"

He backed down the ladder. "I was thinking you could come out to dinner with me."

"Dinner." She had been working with Lisa most of the afternoon as they finalized the menu and she was actually very ready to get out of the house. Of course, with him, it made it special. "Okay. Where are we going to go?"

"I was thinking if we go now while we still have daylight outside, we grab something to go and eat it on the boat."

She loved going with him on the boat. "That sounds perfect."

"Awesome. Then let's hit the road. You just figure out what it is you want to drive through for pickup and we'll head straight to the boat."

Thirty minutes later, they were on the boat. She looked over at him as he drove. The wind ruffled through his combination gray and dark hair. He was so handsome.

He looked over at her. "I'm glad you came."

"I'm glad you invited me. It's been a unique week, hasn't it? I mean, here we are, finalizing what it will take to get the inn open. You'll finish the gazebo and then they'll do the final landscaping around it, and we're ready to open. On top of that, Dallas is now that beautiful girl's helper. He's out there, making sure she has what she needs."

"It's a *very* unique week. Dallas's situation really makes it so."

"It does. He hasn't gone into full detail but told me she isn't in need of anything since she has a ranch and income. She had just moved to the ranch the baby's daddy left her, but she needed help around the place, so now he's going to stay around and help her. I think it's a good thing for him because if he's out there taking care of her stuff and concentrating on helping her, then he has something that helps him not think so much about his own situation. Maybe it will help him get used to not competing. I'm just very curious to see what happens."

"I think it's very interesting myself," Seth said. "Dallas is a great guy to help out like he is. That's a heck of a ranch out there. "

"I know. I had no idea until he told me. The baby's dad had his horses and cattle, but he made his main money off of something he invented for a machine."

"That's really interesting."

"Very. I'm glad Dallas is helping her." They had driven pretty far out onto the ocean, and they could see the coastline in the distance and other boats enjoying the evening. She studied it, took a deep breath, and relaxed. "In a week, I'm going to have the bed-and-breakfast and a restaurant opened. I get chills just thinking about it."

He slowed the boat and then eased it to a halt. They were each in a seat but not that far from each other. He turned his seat toward her and smiled.

"That's one reason I wanted you to come out here and eat with me today. I wanted to see how you were doing on all that. And I know that I'll be finished working for you by the end of this week. It will feel weird. But I want to help you do anything you need done. I'm excited for you and I'm coming to the opening. I think it's going to be a great evening."

"It's still hard to believe I'm here. I can get teary-eyed thinking about everything I've been through, but I'm moving on from all that. I'm putting everything in the past. And I know that I've said this numerous times, but William would be proud that I'm moving on. It's going to be a great night. All the kids are going to get to be there and then friends and anyone who wants to drop in since it is an open house. The invitation will be in the paper also. The party's food will be awesome. It will hopefully be a great night, and I'm so glad you are coming."

He reached across and took her hand. "I'm glad you invited me. I'm glad I was involved in getting it ready. But most of all, I'm glad I've gotten to meet you. You're going to do amazing."

She smiled gently. "I think I'm going to believe you."

He chuckled. "Smart decision. Now, let's grab that bag over there and have us some supper."

"Sounds like a plan to me. And I hope that after

you are not working for me that I still get to come on the boat rides with you every once in a while."

He put his other hand over her hands and held her gaze. "I'm glad to hear you say that because yes, I want to continue our boat rides, and I want to continue seeing you."

"Me too. I know it's a slow process with me getting my life going, but I really enjoy seeing you."

"And that's what I want to hear. Now let's eat."

* * *

The morning after they had come home from the hospital, Lorna was moving slow but she was moving. She stared out the window and watched Dallas mowing her yard—although she still had a hard time calling it her yard. But Dallas was amazing. She knew she needed to be careful with the way she liked him so much. It wasn't just that she was grateful to him; she also needed to be careful that she didn't get liking him and being grateful to him confused.

He had spent the night in the room on the other side of Landon's room. And had come to check on her and the baby whenever he heard her up and she assumed—or had a feeling—a couple of times when she wasn't up. Because she had no one to be there and it was the first night, he had suggested that she let him do that and she had gladly agreed. When she had woken up this morning, he had had breakfast ready. He had told her to spend as much time in bed as she needed to and that he would take care of everything and he would make lunch and supper. She was sad to say, but today she was very sore and didn't know whether this was normal for most new mothers, but she was going to have to take it easy.

Now as she filled her glass with water and stared out the window at him, she sent up a quick prayer of thanks. He was an amazing person. She turned the water off and then went back to her chair in the living room and placed the glass on the table beside it. She sank down into the chair and pulled the blanket over her legs and up to her waist. She picked the glass up and took a long drink. She was breastfeeding a baby and was determined to be hydrated. After finishing a feeding session, she replenished with water. She set her glass down, leaned her head back, closed her eyes and kind of just relaxed. And as crazy as it was, her thoughts kept going to Dallas.

Dallas. She kept telling herself to not go overboard. But right now, her brain was going where it wanted to go, thinking of the nice, handsome man who was her rescuer.

Moments later, she heard the door open. She opened her eyes to see Dallas entering the kitchen. He lifted his hand and then waved to her and strode to the kitchen sink. He turned on the water, grabbed the soap and squirted some into his hands, and started washing them.

"How you doing? You ready for something to eat?" he asked, looking at her.

Her pulse raced. "I'm doing pretty good. I had this wonderful breakfast this morning and I think it just did miracles."

He laughed. "Well then, we're going to see if lunch can do the same thing. Although it's going to be another one of those sandwiches."

"That's okay. It's good."

He turned the water off, got a towel, and wiped his hands off. "I'm going to go to the grocery store after we eat. Well, first I'm going to finish the rest of this yard around the house. There is a lot more for me to mow later but going to the grocery store is more important. I'm going to get us some groceries, so you have the energy you need. I was thinking after we eat, and I go back out there and finish mowing the backyard, that you could write me a list. Keep in mind that you need to build your energy. Any kind of food that you can think that will help do that, we need to get. I can cook on the grill or I can cook in the skillet. I'll look at the list and if there are other things I can think of while I'm there, I'll get it. Put everything you can think of on it. And if you don't have the money for it, I do."

Shock shot through her as he offered to actually take care of her with money. "No, he left me money too, so I'm good. But thank you for the sweet offer. You're amazing. I just don't know what I'd be doing if you weren't here."

"Look, I'm actually grateful to be here. My shoulder is in a bad way. And if I wasn't here, I'd be sitting around, sad about not being at a rodeo and knowing I need to make a life change. Being here helping you is really a good thing for me. Please don't feel bad about it, okay? It's kind of wild to have turned out the way it did. I'm just grateful to have been there to help you and to help you now."

He was totally serious, she could tell by the look on his face. One of the reasons why she really liked him. "Thank you. Thank you very much."

CHAPTER EIGHT

On Sunday afternoon, Alice loaded up her car with a casserole and a baby gift that she had bought the day before, and headed out to the ranch where Lorna lived. She was so proud of her son. Dallas had just come through for this girl, and she was so happy to see it. He had needed this as much as it looked like Lorna needed him. Alice was glad she had pulled back and given them the time alone.

She was excited to see Lorna again and the baby. And to see how Lorna and Dallas were getting along. They knew she was coming and she hoped she wasn't messing up any schedule. She'd pulled the car onto the driveway that led a short distance to the house. The ranch looked pretty.

She had briefly looked up on the internet and seen that the baby's dad had died from cancer, and Dallas told her that it was something he'd had but that it was fast-acting. He was already dying when he had met Lorna. He had come to Houston to sell a few horses when they met. Obviously, they had hit it off, and she had ended up pregnant. They hadn't continued dating after he flown back here but she'd called him with the information. He'd been shocked and revealed he didn't have too long to live. Alice didn't know all the details but he'd left Lorna the ranch and money. He'd taken care of her and his child. Alice was still amazed by the story.

She reached the house, parked the car, and got out. She stared at the large ranch-style home. It was a single story and spread out, with large windows and lots of wood. *Pretty.* She reached in the back seat and pulled out the casserole and the baby's gift, then headed toward the front door. She rang the bell.

Moments later, Dallas answered the door. "Mom, great to see you. Come on in." He pulled the door back and hugged her, then motioned down the hall where she could see into a beautiful living area.

"I'm glad to see you and see the baby and Lorna. I'm glad I got to come out here."

"To tell you the truth, Lorna is very excited about you coming. She's got the baby in the living room for you to meet." He took the casserole from her and closed the door, and they headed down the hall.

The house was very masculine but nice, and when they entered the living room, she saw Lorna in a beige chair with an ottoman. It looked very comfortable and she had a feeling that Lorna spent most of her time in it.

"Mrs. McIntyre, please come in and have a seat right here." Lorna pointed to the seat near her. "I'll let you hold Landon."

Alice crossed the room quickly and sank into the chair that was about a foot from Lorna's. It looked as though it had been moved closer just for her. "Do you know how glad I am to see that y'all are doing well? And this sweet baby is adorable."

"Thank you." Lorna looked across the room at Dallas, who was now headed toward the kitchen. She looked back at Alice. "I couldn't have done this without your son. He's been amazing. I had no one. I was planning on hiring somebody to be here, but I still had two weeks to go and I hadn't gotten it done."

Alice reached her hand out and patted Lorna's arm. "Things work out how they're supposed to. We might not always be happy about how things turn out, but sometimes we're very happy and they work out very well. It looks like this is one of those times. You needed someone who could take care of you and this beautiful little boy and this wonderful place you have out here. And my sweet son over there, who I know is being quiet, needed to be here because of his shoulder. He's got a lot of things he's having to make decisions about, and this is obviously the perfect place for him to be. I don't know, but you know, some things just work out."

"Yes, they do. Now, would you like to hold this little boy?"

"I would love to. I've been expecting a grandchild myself eventually, but nobody's gotten married yet, so I haven't gotten to experience one of my own. But right now, I'm excited about holding this beautiful fella."

She accepted the baby as Lorna handed him over, and she cuddled him close. She smiled down at him, he was wonderful. He was sleeping but opened his eyes and looked at her, and then closed them again. "He's adorable. I always loved holding my babies. I hope you don't mind me coming over every once in a while. And honestly, I'm getting the restaurant and bed-and-breakfast opened right now, but I won't be working there every day. I have plenty of people hired, so if you ever need anything or you might like to do something and have someone come watch him, I would be more than happy to do it."

She saw the shock on the girl's face. This young woman was alone; having left where she'd lived and moved here to a town that was completely new to her clearly had been hard.

"I don't know what to say…thank you."

"Don't look so shocked. I'm really glad to have met you, and I consider you a friend now. I hope you will consider me a friend."

"Yes. I can use a friend," Lorna said, with a soft emotion filling her words.

Alice rocked the baby. "I can tell you that there are others who will love being your friend. One is Lisa, who helped get your bed ready. She wanted to come but she's panicking as she gets ready for Friday's open house and the official opening on Saturday, so she didn't come. But she will. And there will be others too."

"I hope she gets everything done. She sounds like she works very hard."

"She does. But it will be done. She's just a perfectionist and her food is the best. You know, I'm not sure if you're getting around all that much yet, but you're welcome to come to the opening. Dallas is supposed to come, and I'm sure you're welcome to join him. Of course, I know you might be worried about the baby, so it just depends on if you want to bring the baby out."

Dallas came back into the room and took a seat on the couch, leaning forward with his elbows on his knees. "And I'd be glad for you to go with me, if you thought you felt like it. But I know it would depend on the baby and how you're feeling."

"It sounds so wonderful. I would love to see the B&B. I'm feeling stronger every day, as it's been almost a week. However, I don't think the baby would be ready to come out by then. I think I'll have to call it off for that night and maybe after Landon's a little older I can come out. It just sounds really nice."

"Okay," Alice said. "It's always open. You just let me know and we'll have lunch together and check it out and walk on the beach if you want. But maybe not."

"Yes, I think I'll skip the walk on the beach this time." Lorna grinned.

* * *

By Friday, minutes before the event, Alice was pleased that the inn looked charming. The patio and gardens were outstandingly beautiful. They had tables set up and the amazing food Lisa and her helpers had prepared was set out. The staff looked happy and she had been very happy with each one she had hired. She was even more thrilled now that they were here, and she knew they would be awesome greeting guests.

The pavilion was just perfect tonight. It would

have some great moments over the years with special events. Tonight, the band that she had hired had set up there and would play all evening and if guests wanted to dance, they could. The dining room inside was stunning. They had set it up so people could eat after they'd picked from the food being served in the garden area. It would be used for visiting and enjoyment later when the restaurant opened and it would hold a good number of people. Also, with the outdoor patio area, it would hold even more. She loved it. And so did Lisa.

Alice checked her watch and took a deep breath. She knew that Lisa and her people were busy in the kitchen, getting the last things ready, and they were busy outside setting up the food. They were all keeping busy. It was going to be a great night. She heard a knock on the door of the back area and turned to see Seth. Her heart jumped. She was so glad to see him. She rushed to the door, opened it and walked into his arms. It was just natural. She looked up at him, glad his arms were around her, holding her close. He was encouraging her but in that moment she knew that she had gone a long way in her feelings for him.

"I'm so glad to see you."

He grinned. "I'm excited to see you. And it looks like I got here early enough to see you and encourage you before everybody else arrives. I'm sorry but I had to say that." He was looking into her eyes and she patted him on the back.

"I actually needed you here. Everything's looking great and I'm very excited, but I have a little bit of nerves going on. You are definitely helping me settle down."

He kissed her forehead. "I'll do whatever I need to help you feel better, honey. You look beautiful. And everything looks fantastic." He squeezed her hard and then just kept one arm around her so they could both stare out at the gorgeous garden area with the ocean in the background. "It's great, Alice—just beautiful. Everybody's going to have a good time. I see the band over there getting ready. That will be fun. And if you decide you want to dance, I am your man. I know you're going to be busy but I'm letting you know I am available if you decide to take a spin."

"I don't know…who knows, I might end up taking you up on that offer. I think everybody's going to enjoy it. The inside of the house looks wonderful, and we have a couple of young women inside to show anybody around who wants to look around. But people are welcome to walk around and look on their own, too. Then the helpers will make sure nobody has messed up the beds or done anything crazy like that, you know what I mean?" She rolled her eyes and frowned, teasing.

He laughed. "I hadn't thought about that, but you could be right. People or couples might decide to test the bed out."

She was being silly, and it felt good as it helped relax her. "Oh, there is always a chance someone does that, but I doubt it. Yet, one never knows."

He laughed again and squeezed her shoulder. "Well, let's think positive. All right, anything I can help you do?"

"Sure. I think it's going to get busy soon—you can just help me welcome people and if someone needs directions to anything, you can sure tell them how to get there. And I'll be pointing out to everyone that you did most of the work and that you are open for business."

"All right. I didn't come for that but I'm always open to new customers."

"Well, you know, you are dedicated, talented, and a hard worker, so it is not anything that shouldn't be bragged about. I hope you get some customers from tonight."

"Thank you. And I hope that anything I did to help make the place look good will help you get customers."

They smiled at each other and then the doorbell rang.

"Uh oh, I hear the first doorbell. Somebody's

here." Seth turned them toward the door. "Should you answer it?"

Her pulse pounding, Alice shook her head just as the voice of the girl who was in control of the front door welcomed people.

"To keep me from standing at the front door all night, I decided that I would welcome people from here."

"Makes sense."

Jackson and Nina walked out the door to them and each hugged her, then Nina hugged Seth, and Jackson shook his hand and patted him on the shoulder.

"It looks beautiful and amazing," Nina said, clearly in awe.

"It is, and it should be a great evening," Jackson said.

"And so many people are coming. I've heard people talking about it all week," Nina said.

"I hope so. And I am so glad to see you two."

"Hey, we're here," Riley said as he walked up to her, grinning. He threw his arms around her and hugged her and then side-stepped so Tucker, who was with him, could do the same.

"It's going to be a great night," Riley said. "And I see a lot of good food, so that means that Lisa must be around. She can cook! I was looking forward to coming just for her cooking."

Everybody laughed and Alice patted his chest. "Well, you are a good tester, so you can let me know what you think after you've tried everything. It would be very helpful."

He laughed. "I'll be happy to do that, Mom. I like helping you."

"I'll join him." Tucker laughed. "This looks awesome, Mom."

"Thank you," she said, smiling bigger. "Now, just enjoy yourselves and if anybody looks like they need help finding their way, please show them the right direction—that would be great." She was so very glad to see her family. All were there but Dallas.

"It's awesome, Mom," Dallas said with perfect timing as he'd come from the garden entrance.

She spun and hugged him. "You got to come! Yeah. And thank you. I'm very pleased with it. How is Lorna doing?"

"She's doing good. She's made a lot of progress this week. She said to wish you well. She wanted to come but she just wasn't ready to bring the baby around so many people or find someone to watch him. I don't blame her but thank you for inviting her."

Alice was glad she'd invited her and hopefully made her feel welcome. "I understand. I'm so happy she's doing better. You being out there is a good thing."

"Thanks. I'm glad to be able to help her."

More people were arriving, and Alice sighed and looked at her family with a smile. "Okay, family, y'all go enjoy yourselves and I'll go greet other people. Love y'all."

And so the evening began.

Lots of people showed up. Lisa came out and joined her in greeting people after she had made sure things in the kitchen were going well. It was evident she had hired a good crew and she had some free time because people wanted to meet both Alice and Lisa.

"Hey, glad you joined me." Alice gave her a hug.

"I'm glad to join you. It looks like it's going to be a busy night. This is very promising for the future," Lisa said.

"Yes, it is, and Lisa, I'm so very glad you are in this with me."

Lisa put her arm around her. "You have no idea how happy I am to be here. This is going to be amazing. And I am looking forward to it, with everything in me."

"Me too. Starting over is exciting. I'm so glad I decided to do it. It was like William kind of led the way out here, and I know he's happy for me tonight."

"I agree. I totally agree."

Alice looked around the gardens, where everyone

visited and some people were dancing. Her eyes spotted Seth visiting with Dallas. She was so glad he was here. His gaze met hers and he smiled, lifting his glass to her. Her heart beat faster as she smiled at him.

And she knew in more ways than just the B&B opening that this was a great new beginning.

CHAPTER NINE

Nina was full of excitement for Alice and Lisa. "I think this has been a wonderful evening and I'm so happy for your mom and for Lisa," she said, leaning close to Jackson.

"I am too, and you know I've been taking everything in and though finding a wedding date is starting to look like the hardest thing in the world, we will do it. But finding where we want to have it doesn't have to be as hard. This would be a beautiful place for a wedding, although I don't know how many people you want to invite, so it might not fit everybody."

She put her arms around him and he started swaying as if they were on the dance floor. She smiled and leaned into him, looking up into his face, so happy. "I think it's a gorgeous place, but don't you want to have it on the ranch?"

He kissed her briefly. "We have a very pretty garden at the ranch, but I want it only if you do."

"I think it's where it should be."

"What's where it should be?" Riley asked, coming up.

They stopped swaying and Nina smiled at him. "We're discussing getting married. We've decided the wedding is going to be at the ranch."

Riley smiled. "I think that's a great idea. It's a perfect place, where we can set up the big tent like Dad used to do for cattle promotions. I like the idea."

"I think we have a plan." Jackson gave her another kiss.

She was thrilled they'd come to agreement on that. Now to figure out the date. She looked at Riley, having been told by Jackson that he'd gone to a camp over the weekend. "How was your weekend?"

Jackson cocked his head. "Yeah, how'd it go?"

"Well, it was fine. I was on the run a pretty good bit, fixing different problems that kind of rise up when you've got over fifty campers, all women. I was busy, but I got to see a lot of stuff. They fish, they get facials and massages and had hot tubs, among other things. They went on these nighttime studies of the moon and stars that they seemed to really enjoy. They had a social gathering each evening and a fun dance, just the ladies all dancing in a big group to fun music—you know, partying together. They did a lot."

"It sounds like it," Nina said. "What was your favorite?"

He laughed. "There was a lot of personal woman stuff going on and the massages were all different kinds. I wasn't supposed to see the massages—they were held behind a large set of temporary wooden barriers. They put this mud all over them and then they would lay in the sun and it would dry. Not all of them did that one, but anyway, it was very interesting."

"Sounds interesting." Jackson grinned. "But if you weren't supposed to see it, how did you?"

"Oh, I was the handyman, and one of their tank engines stopped and so I had to go behind the curtains used to keep the area from view of the whole group areas. Though most everyone was covered up while I was working, there were a couple who were covered in mud and figured that was enough."

Everyone laughed.

"Yeah, anyway, I'm checking more into this. I just think that we could make a camp work, or I could, since I know nobody else is interested in it. But I just have this thought in my head about doing it. I think it could be a huge success and you know it won't always have to be that. It could be a regular campground, but this is just an added, say, once-a-month something. I don't know. I'm very interested and there's a lot of women who love it."

"Well, I think it's pretty cool," Nina said. "I'm thinking about the lady. The one you met at the gas station who was coming back from one of these. The one who got your interest up. Was she there?"

He looked disappointed. "No, she wasn't. I don't know if I'll ever see her again but she got me interested in this just by meeting her, so I figure if I do this, maybe at some point, I'll meet her again." He smiled. "I know it's crazy, but I just can't help myself."

Jackson gave him a grin. "Hey, you never know. When it's meant to be, it's meant to be. I met this one going around a corner here because her cute little dog didn't want to stay home. Just that one little thing. So, you open this camp and she may show up. It could be a romance that leads to a marriage."

"Agree." Nina kissed him on the cheek.

Riley laughed. "Yup, you never know. Anyway, I'm still seriously thinking about it, so y'all get ready."

"It could be a big success, Riley. Just look at what Mom's done," Jackson said. "What Lisa has done. Look at all these people here tonight—they're having a great time. Think about the people who will come and stay the weekend or the week, and the people who just like to come eat at that very cool restaurant that amazes me. Lisa—whew, that woman can cook."

"Yes, she can," Nina said. "They're going to do great, and me meeting them was a blessing that led to you. I'm very grateful to have met them. It will be kind of strange when I move out to the ranch and I don't have the place next door so I can't come over and have coffee and snacks with them."

"I'll bet you come see them often," Jackson said. "The ranch is out in the boonies and you won't see as many friends out there, so I know they'll want you to visit them."

"How many months before you set the date?" Riley asked again.

She smiled. "We're still trying to decide. We can't decide if we want to have it sooner while it's a little bit chilly or if we want to wait until the spring. We could have it within six weeks and it would still be warm." She smiled at Jackson.

Riley watched them. "Why not go for it?"

Jackson grinned. "I'm not sure but I'm getting the feeling that we're going to have a wedding in about six weeks if we can find a date."

Nina smiled knowing this was what she wanted. "Hopefully we can and if not, we will just invite you and whoever can make it." She might be selfish thinking that way, but right now, looking at her man, that was how she felt.

CHAPTER TEN

"Are you ready?" Dallas asked Lorna a few days after the opening of his mom's inn. Lorna had been getting stronger and the baby was doing great. He was holding him at the moment. Dallas was crazy about this little boy. He grinned at him, and it made Dallas grin back.

"He likes you. And no wonder—you're very good to him."

Dallas looked up and smiled at Lorna. "I think he likes everybody. Not that he's seen a lot of people, but I think he would. So anyway, are you ready to head out for a little ranch ride?"

"I am. We've been so closed in and I'm ready to go look. And maybe you can talk to me about this. I'm still so confused."

"I know, but I have to tell you that it's a great

place. I mean, I talked to somebody down at the feed store the other day and they said that Lewis was worried about his ranch and that he had already set it up in his will to be sold and the money be donated to something. Then you came in the picture, and it's a good thing. I mean, I hate that the guy died but it ended up working out for you with the baby. And I have a feeling he was glad to have someone special to leave all this to. I haven't seen your account books but from what you've told me, y'all are set up for life. And I'm sure the guy was glad to have someone to leave it to."

She sighed. "I hope so. It's true; he had a lot of money that he got for that part he invented. It's invested, so that adds up. I mean, it's worth a good amount and growing. And then the ranch is a nice place to live. Let's go look at it and we'll talk some more. I'm just ready to get out of the house. And Landon is too."

They went out to his truck and he held the handle of the baby's car seat with one hand as he opened the door for Lorna. Which he held her elbow as she climb up into the truck. She didn't even have any trouble this time.

"You did that well," he said after she had gotten into the seat and he was still holding the door.

She looked at him and smiled. "I'm very pleased. I

feel like I have regained myself. And I got on the scale this morning and I'm actually now my original weight. Though it's not all back where it belongs. I've lost weight in some places and gained weight in others."

He hitched a brow at her. "Well, it didn't look to me like you gained anything."

"I had actually gained twenty pounds, but then I have lost everything but twelve pounds after the delivery. The rest has fallen off naturally, I think from me feeding my sweet boy."

"Probably so. You're doing good. And you are gaining your energy back, and that's great." He smiled, then closed the door and went around to his side and latched the baby carrier into the seat behind him. He then closed the door and climbed into his own seat. He had enjoyed every day he had been here with Lorna. He liked her very much.

He headed the truck out down the pasture road and over one of many cattle guards. "The guy had obviously not liked to get out of his truck and open a gate. There are cattle guards everywhere. It's very nice."

"Wow, that's great," she said.

"Yeah, instead of having to stop and open gates, he set all of the gates up as cattle guards, which is really great for you. You can just drive over them and if you need to get the cows through, you open the gate down the fence there."

"That's nice. It's pretty, isn't it?" She looked at the pastures with the cattle and there were a few horses mingling.

"Very. You not only inherited a very well-designed ranch but a very pretty place. And it's about time to hire some help and gather these small calves up for sale. I talked to several sales barns around town and found out which one he liked to use, and they have a sale coming up. It's in a couple of weeks, so I have to ask you if you want to do that? It's a normal thing and the man I talked to said that Lewis usually sold cattle and calves at every sale. Because his cattle breed at different times."

She studied the cattle and then looked at him. "Well, can you do that? I mean, will you have time to do that or do I need to start looking for someone to hire?"

He did not want her to hire somebody, because he was enjoying what he was doing too much. "No, I'm here and I'm enjoying helping you, and I know how to sell cows. Growing up working a huge ranch means I've been to many cattle sales before the miracle of the oil strikes. For years, just me and my brothers did the work. While I was competing in bull riding, I was still working on the ranch. When they hit oil and it changed our lives to billionaire status."

"The billionaire status," she said, sounding stunned.

"Yes, it's a lot to take in. So anyway, when they hired ranch workers, I went to competing in bull riding full-time. I'm pretty positive my days of doing that are over." He slowed and looked out over the cattle. "It's getting more obvious to me."

"You've been thinking about that, haven't you?"

He took a deep breath and looked over at her. "Yes. I know I need to. I didn't really want to accept it. But I don't want to be a crippled man in my older years. And yes, I've thoroughly enjoyed myself as a competing bull rider. But, I have to look at it seriously and to be honest, you've helped me with that in a huge way. Being out here and helping you, my shoulder has improved. Yes, it still has a ways to go, but it's so much better out here, helping you and that cute little baby back there."

"I am so glad. I hate it for you but you don't want to make it a lifetime injury when it doesn't have to be."

"True. I'm grateful to you. And I've enjoyed what I've done, but I look at your ranch and I think about what I can do to help you improve it more. Get you going out here is one of those things, because you don't really know what's going on. I mean, since you've never really owned a ranch before. And I do love ranching. I just also love riding bulls."

"I'd hate to see you hurt yourself where you can't do what you enjoy. But I watch you out here working—yes, I do sometimes watch you out the window—and it's clear you really enjoy working in the yard, working with the horses and checking on the cattle."

"Yes, I do. I can't help myself."

"Well then, while you continue to make your personal decision, I would love if you sold the cattle for me. And I'll try to watch what you do so when you go find what you're going to do for yourself, after you move on from the rodeo, I'll know more about what I need to do."

His chest squeezed at the mention of going and doing something else, because he knew he would be very glad to continue doing what he was doing. He really enjoyed helping her and the baby. He enjoyed every moment he was around them. And he was glad to introduce her to her ranch.

He topped the hill and paused as a lake came into view. He smiled at her. "Did you know you had this beauty?"

Her mouth fell open, looking at the lake in front of them. "No, I didn't. It is gorgeous and big."

He smiled, pleased. "It's not gigantic, but yeah,

it's a very nice lake. The cattle like it when they are in this area. But you could enjoy it too. There's a nice fishing pier. And it has a bench on it. Do you want to go over there and sit for a few minutes?"

"That'd be nice. I can't believe this is here."

"Well, you've got to remember this is not a real small ranch. No, it's not as big as the one my family owns but having a two-hundred-thousand-acre ranch is kind of unusual. This ranch, with what I'm guessing is around twenty thousand or so acres, is great. It's a nice size to raise cattle. And horses too. I was in the office in the barn and looking over some papers on the desk. Sorry, I couldn't help myself. But Lewis raised the horses and sold them too. Some of them he was training but some of the colts he raised and sold as they were. So he was just enjoying himself and making money. You can do that too."

"If I can get used to it."

"I think you can." He parked the truck a few feet from the pier and they got out. He got the baby's carrier out and Landon was smiling as he looked up at Dallas. "Hey, cute fella. You are about to see a lake. One you may fish in one day."

They walked toward the pier and he put his free hand under Lorna's elbow to make sure she didn't fall considering the ground wasn't exactly straight. When they made it to the wooden pier, they walked down it.

The bench was perfect for two people and he set the baby on the pier, looking up at them, as they sat down.

"So, what do you think?" He watched the amazed expression on her face and smiled.

"I love it. I love it a lot."

He grinned, because it was obvious. "I thought you'd say that, so that's why we came this way today. We could have gone the opposite way and I could have showed you the other side of the ranch but I figured this would be your favorite spot."

"You seem to know me." She smiled at him.

He couldn't help himself and reached out and patted her hand, which was lying on her thigh. "You're going to enjoy this place once we get everything in line and you're used to it. And the baby will love growing up here. It's very nice."

Lorna flipped her hand over beneath his and folded her fingers through his. She looked at him with emotional eyes. "I'm feeling very blessed right now."

"And you should. This is a great place. And it will provide for you and your baby."

She squeezed his hand. "No, I'm feeling very blessed because you showed up in my life. And I'll be sad when you decide to leave. But right now, I'm so happy."

He lifted his other hand, cupped her cheek, and smiled at her. "Don't worry. I don't think we were connected for no reason. Our situations help each other too much, so I'm not pulling out and running off anytime soon. Unless you send me." Unable to stop himself, he ran his fingers down her jaw, wanting with everything in him to kiss her. Instead, he pulled his hand away because he knew he was inching toward trouble.

Her eyes softened. You just made me very happy."

CHAPTER ELEVEN

Alice led the couple who had just checked in up the stairs and down the hall to the room named the Pelican Room. She opened the door and turned to smile at them. "I hope you enjoy it. Now let's get you inside and if you have any problems, you just give us a call. If I'm not here, then there will be someone downstairs who can take care of you. The restaurant is open for breakfast, lunch, and dinner." She told them the times. "They are also listed there on the desk there in the corner."

"Thank you. It is just lovely, and we're really looking forward to our time here," the woman said, and her husband agreed.

"You are very welcome. And thank you for choosing the Star Gazer Inn." Alice walked back down the stairs, loving what she was doing. They had been open a week and everything had gone well.

They had had a few small kinks but not much. It was normal to have a few things needing to be adjusted during opening week. Especially in the cleaning and setup of the rooms. Not much had gone wrong and had been easily fixed. When she got downstairs, she walked down the hall to the kitchen. The helpers were cooking and she found Lisa sitting at her desk in the small office and going over what looked like the menu. She hadn't taken any time off.

"Hey, how's your day going?" Lisa asked.

Alice sat down across the desk from her. "Pretty good. I've had a fun week and I just wanted to come tell you that you have done an outstanding job."

Lisa smiled at her. "Thank you. I have thoroughly enjoyed myself and just think this is going to be a great winning situation that we've come up with. I'm glad you asked me to join you."

"You are a blessing to me. I came in to remind you that I have an art show to go to on Saturday. Are you sure you don't want to go?"

"I would like to go, but I would rather be here and make sure everything's going well. I understand completely that you need to go. So, you just represent us both. I know Nina's going to do well. And Jackson will be there with her, and it will be great. She's so talented. People who come here always comment on her pictures."

"So true. Okay, we have a plan, and Seth is going to go with me."

"That's wonderful news. Y'all have not seen as much of each other since he's not working here. This will be good."

"Yes, it will be. I've thoroughly enjoyed getting the inn open and everything involved but I've missed seeing him every day. It's taking a little getting used to that fact. He's texted me and called me but hasn't overdone it. He doesn't want to take up my time and mess up my opening. But I miss him and can tell he feels the same way for me."

"So how are you feeling about that?"

"I'm becoming more and more aware that my emotions are opening wide."

Lisa looked encouraging with her gentle smile. "I think that's wonderful. And I'm not going to bring it up all the time, but I just know that your sweet William would have been happy for you. And your kids, they will be too. They're very encouraging to you."

"Yes. So, anyway, we've got our dream open here and it's doing great every night. I'm amazed we've had a full house in the restaurant and that's because of you—you're amazing. And then the bed-and-breakfast had almost a full house all week, so I think that's wonderful."

"I agree."

"God's been good to us. And anyway, I'm not going to feel guilty when I leave Saturday for the art show with Seth. I'm really looking forward to it. I know that Nina is going to have a great art show. And you are going to make sure everything is good here."

The front phone began to ring. "Oops, I better go answer the phone—it's my morning. So talk to you later."

"Thanks for coming to visit." Lisa smiled and winked at her. "It's going to only get better. And you're going to have a wonderful evening tomorrow."

"I totally agree." Alice hurried up the hallway. She couldn't wait until tomorrow.

* * *

Lisa watched Alice leave and she felt so happy for her. Then she went back to work, needing to get all her planning done. People were reacting to her food so positively that she wanted to make certain it continued. The restaurant was full every night so far, and lunch was full too. Breakfast was less packed, which gave her a little break, but it was busy.

They had been open a week and she was

overworking, and she knew it, but she would figure things out. She would get her supply orders better organized and not have to spend as much time making calls.

One of her assistants looked in the door. "We have an omelet order."

"Thanks, I'll be right there." She cooked and baked the main dishes so her time in her office was limited. She knew she would probably have to hire some more help, as in another chef. And she hoped when the time came she'd find just the right one.

Moments later, she was preparing the omelet, from the vegetables Zora had chopped up earlier in preparation for the morning orders. "You did a great job of these veggies."

The short-haired younger woman smiled. "Thank you. I've really enjoyed the week and want to make you happy."

"You are doing a great job." She poured the mixture from the mixing bowl onto the small skillet, then she looked around. She had Zora and Lilly as assistants and they were good. Then there were the other kitchen helpers, the dishwashers, and waiters. It looked as if everyone on this shift was in the room. "Everyone, I just want to take this moment to tell you that you're doing a great job. The guests are all happy and that is wonderful. Anyway, keep up the good work and thank you."

There were thank-you calls from everyone as she turned the omelet over and smiled. She was living her dream.

* * *

Nina's nerves were a bit rattled as she stood in the art studio and watched people looking at her work. She was glad to be back to showing her work again after having to be in hiding from the crazy person who messed up her life. However, in hiding out, she had met her sweetheart, Jackson. Now life was getting back to normal and they were trying to plan a wedding, slowly but surely.

Jackson walked up and handed her a drink as a couple came over and began talking to her about her paintings. He said hello and then stood back and let her visit with them. A few moments later, he leaned in and whispered, "Excuse me, I'm going to go talk with Seth and my mom."

She smiled at him. "Okay," she said, and then went back to the conversation with the woman and man as they talked to her about the different paintings. They wanted to know the story behind the paintings as they were obviously trying to figure out which one they wanted. It was a wonderful conversation as she enjoyed telling stories about why she painted certain paintings. It didn't take long for them to realize that they wanted the painting of a man on the hill overlooking the Guadalupe River.

Happy about their decision, she thanked them and then excused herself and went to join the conversation of her family—or soon-to-be family.

Alice threw her arms around Nina and hugged her tight. "This is beautiful. I mean, I love looking at your paintings, but to walk into a room full of them is amazing. And look at all of these people who also are enjoying looking at your work. You are going to do well. Really well."

"I agree." Seth grinned big as he gave her a hug. "I'd buy all of them but I wouldn't have room for all of them."

Jackson put an arm around her shoulders. "I'm going to marry a very talented woman."

"Thank y'all so much. And it is really good to see you out and about," she said to Alice. "The restaurant and B&B are doing amazing. I haven't come over much this week because I've been busy getting this ready, but my goodness, every time I walk out my door, there's someone new there. And the beach behind our homes has more people on it than in the three years I've been here."

Alice chuckled. "I'm very happy, too, but I was glad to leave the B&B and get the chance to come see your art exhibit tonight. And Lisa said to send you her best wishes and her congratulations, but she stayed back to oversee everything. She's very determined."

Nina agreed with her. "After what she has been through, this being a success is extremely important to her. I mean, it was extremely important to you too, but you know it's kind of a little bit of a different situation. It's just going to be successful and we needed it. Our little end of the beach was kind of lonesome without the inn being open."

"I agree," Alice said. "So, I see people coming to talk to you, so me and my handsome escort are going to walk around and enjoy the pictures and let you talk to your admirers."

Nina grinned. "Okay, but we'll get together later, or I hope we can. If not, it's great to have y'all here."

She watched them turn and saw Alice's hand in the crook of Seth's arm. She looked at Jackson. "I wonder how long it's going to be before they are, you know, connected. Getting married maybe."

He smiled. "Well, I think they're connected. I never really thought I could see my mom with anybody but my dad, but I've gotten used to them being together. I can see where it's helping Mom, and I guess God just made it to where you could love someone with all your heart and then when they were gone, miraculously it could happen again."

She grabbed his arm and hugged him. "Yes, it's kind of a miracle, I think."

* * *

By the end of the week, Dallas had hired a couple of ranch hands to work a few times a week. He had them helping herd the cattle all to the same pasture today. He had looked at the property lines on the property survey. He and Lorna had realized that this ranch had twenty thousand acres, which was certainly not gigantic like his family ranch. This was a size that in central Texas would be considered a really nice-sized ranch and as weird as it sounded, he actually preferred it to the gigantic ranch his family owned, with nearly two hundred thousand acres. They had to have tons of land when it was just him and his brothers growing up. And having to deal with it mostly by themselves, it was hard work. But after they had grown up and were getting out of high school and into college, they had struck oil—lots of oil.

Life had changed and that was when he had gotten to go full-time into his dream of rodeo. And after he had lived all those years working as hard as he had and being as healthy as he was, it had been hard when he had been thrown from that bull, then stomped, rolled on, and stomped again. His whole body had been injured, but most of it had been his shoulder. Everything recovered but his shoulder just had never fully healed. His doctors had warned him that it certainly might not heal all the way and that continuing his bull riding, with all the strain, could only make it worse.

Anyway, he was seeing results being here and from babying his shoulder, being very careful with it. And though he could do things with it now that he couldn't do when they first started—he wasn't in as bad a shape—would he get back to being fully recovered?

As they gathered the cattle into the pasture, he kept thinking about his future and what he wanted from it. As crazy as it sounded, he had been drawn to Lorna immediately and it hadn't stopped. At first, he had been worried that it was just infatuation. Or was it the need he had in him to help people? He tried to tell himself it wasn't that he was just infatuated with her beauty or intrigued by her story. He had tried to tell himself that he needed to give it time. But he had been here five weeks and they were getting ready to have this sale over the weekend. He knew this was where he belonged, and if Lorna happened to have feelings for him, he didn't want to bring it up too soon. So he was working and trying as hard as possible to not be an idiot. To not run her off. In his mind, he could see that she had feelings for him. But then there was the other part thinking that maybe she was just grateful to him. That was the worrisome part, the part that made him fear that asking or starting something too early would be a huge mistake.

So he rode out into the pasture where the cows were, and he and the guys went through and separated out the ones that were of the right age to sell and the ones that weren't quite there and still needed a little longer. And he forced himself to let his thoughts go back to work and not on the woman he knew he loved.

CHAPTER TWELVE

By the end of the third week in business, Lisa knew she needed another chef. They had been very busy, and though she didn't work every hour, she worked most of them. She took off after breakfast when she could, and in the afternoon, she took off a couple of hours before four because they opened at six and she had to get ready. They had decided that being open all day long would be pushing it, at least at first, so they had decided on these limited hours. Thankfully, it had enabled her to have a little rest.

However, now she knew that seven days a week was too much for her with all these hours. It was aggravating, but it was the truth. She loved being here but her body didn't, so she put out some job notices last week. She had already had a meeting yesterday with a young woman who she wasn't greatly impressed with, so she was hoping she would have better luck with the others who had applied so far. She hoped to hire a woman and not have to contend with a man. However, a well-known male chef had applied, and she'd been shocked and intrigued to see his name. She was interviewing him today.

She was in her small office area when Libby, the desk clerk for the day, led Zane Tyson into the room. Libby smiled at her and lifted a brow that only Lisa could see and then left. She knew why Libby was smiling like that: because Zane was one undeniably handsome guy and he was muscular, very well built.

"Hello." He smiled and her stomach did crazy things.

"Hello." She forced her voice to be business-like. "Come on in and have a seat. It's nice to meet you, Mr. Tyson."

"Please, call me Zane." He sat, set his elbows on the arms, and studied her. "You have an amazing place here, from what I've seen. And I've heard that it is doing great business. The reviews that I've seen in the paper have been amazing. Plus, I've talked to a lot of people who have eaten here and they say your cooking is awesome."

Stunned by his words, she couldn't help but smile. "I'm thrilled to hear that. I've worked very hard to give people a delicious experience."

"Well, it looks like you have. And when I saw your ad, I was intrigued."

"Where do you work now?"

"I work at Grandberry's." He smiled. "It's been a great place to work but I've kind of gotten bored there. They won't let me change up the menu and I have help, so if I left, I would not hurt them since they don't change their menu ever. And to be honest, I looked at your menu and I was enthralled by it. And I don't have to say it, but your view here is noteworthy also. I don't know…it just looks like a really cool place to work. When I was reading the menus, I just thought it would be a new experience for me, and I would love it. I could, or would be, a big help to you. I am, well, you know…you would say the same thing…I think I'm very good at what I do."

Yes, he was. She had known his name the moment she saw it and she had known his reputation. The only thing that bothered her was that he was a male and she, after what she had been through with her ex, simply wasn't positive she wanted to work with a man. Her other helpers were all women. She just wasn't certain. But he did appeal to her. Not on the man side, she told herself, but on the cooking side and the part that had honestly told her what he liked. He wanted something different and she just had a feeling.

He tilted his head to the side and studied her with

his dark-navy eyes. "Do you have a preference on hiring a man or a woman?"

She sighed. "To be honest, and I assume I probably need to be honest, I was more inspired to hire a woman. I've been through, as you probably know, a very hard and unusual divorce. And I'm not completely in the mood to trust a man. I know that's not fair, but that's just what I'm fighting right now. I also know that it's wrong."

"I've seen others go through this, and I understand. But I can assure you that I'm not a horrible person. I'm not looking to hurt you or give you problems. I'm simply looking for a job that sounds awesome, with an extremely talented chef in an interesting place. This job has it all."

She breathed in deeply and nodded. "I've looked at your papers, your resume, and I've actually, it has been awhile, but I've eaten your food with a friend there at the restaurant you ran. It was very impressive. So anyway, I'm not going to make a decision today. I have a few more interviews this week, but I will give you a call soon to let you know one way or the other."

He nodded and then stood. "All right then, thank you. I just want you to know—well, you probably already know it, since I've got a pretty good reputation from the restaurant I work at—I'm a hard worker and I'll do whatever you need. And I'm not horrible when it comes to being a boss to the people who work for me. Yes, I expect them to give me their best, but I can also be understanding if they're trying really hard. If they're being lazy, I can't put up with it."

She stood and smiled. "Then on that, we're in agreement. Thanks for coming in, and I'll talk to you later in the week."

He turned and left the room, and she sat back down. *Wow, he couldn't just cook; he also was very dedicated, and he had a very good reputation to back him up. Could she be okay with hiring a man?*

She had received more pictures from her ex-husband, and she finally called her lawyer and was letting her lawyer deal with him. Thankfully, for the last three days, she hadn't gotten anything from him, but she wasn't positive that would stay that way unless she actually went through with suing him or whatever her lawyer suggested. Then again, she knew she had to get her life back, and she couldn't let her experience with her ex have her pick or not pick the right chef to regain her life.

It should just be that she hired the best person for the job.

* * *

It had been a beautiful week. Alice had been thrilled as it seemed that their ads were working because their phones were ringing. It wasn't just the guest rooms that were filled; it was also the restaurant. It was doing amazing.

She had hoped that hiring Lisa would be a great decision considering many, many people around this area knew her reputation for cooking, baking, and entertaining. Being married to the jerk she had been married to, a well-known lawyer, she had been involved in the entertaining, dinners, and charities that he had also been involved in. Lisa had cooked and donated her time and food, and it always was loved. Lisa was so very talented.

Alice stood in the garden and looked up at the outside seating area that was full. She walked up the steps and waved when someone waved at her, and then she went inside to the interior dining room. It, too, was pretty much filled. It was amazing. The food was unbelievable.

However, Alice knew that after these past few weeks that Lisa was going to have to hire another chef. Not just a helper but a professional chef who could give her time off. She knew that she had been interviewing, so Alice really hoped something had come out of it. She walked into the kitchen area and saw her friend cooking several dishes on the grill. She walked over and just watched in amazement as Lisa worked. There was no way Alice could ever cook like that. But her friend, this amazing woman, could.

"I am just always amazed to watch you cook."

Lisa smiled at her as she began placing the food onto the waiting plates. One was a grilled chicken and onions, another one was a steak, and another one looked like a fajita chicken dish. After she had the main courses on the dish, her helper took them and began adding the other portions of the meal.

Lisa smiled at her. "Come on, I have a minute, so let's go to my office. Y'all let me know when I need to come back to cook something," she said to her people, and then she led Alice into the small office area. She sat down at her desk and Alice took the guest chair. "So I've interviewed all week. And I have a problem, I think, and I need to ask your opinion."

"Okay, tell me."

"Have you heard of Zane Tyson? He works at Grandberry's, you know, and he's very, very talented. He came in earlier this week and applied."

"Seriously? The man is amazing. He only gets the best reviews. That restaurant stayed busy all the time. Although, from what I know, it hasn't changed in a very long time."

"I thought you would know him. He came in two days ago. I wasn't planning on hiring a man. I just don't know how comfortable I'd be having a man working underneath me or being in charge when I'm not here. But he's an amazing chef, and I can't get him off my mind. What do you think? Out of everybody who applied, he's the best. I'm actually shocked that he applied. But he's looking for something new. They haven't changed their menu in years and he has, I think, a couple of chefs who work for him who could take over with no problem. I'm just torn."

Alice could see it in Lisa's face but she could also see that her friend was drawn very much to the idea of hiring someone good to work for her and the restaurant. "Well, I have never really heard any kind of ugly talk about the man. I know that he does TV shows sometimes and he donates his time a lot. He seems like a very nice guy. And I think that you two would work well together. I know that you've been through some horrible stuff, but not everybody is like that jerk you were married to and doesn't deserve to be judged like it. I think you should give him a try. From what I've see of him, he seems really nice."

Her friend looked down and rubbed her forehead, then looked back up. "That's what I think. I have to not let my past affect my future. And I think he would be really good here. He admires the inn and being on the beach really appealed to him. And though I haven't really met him before this, he did seem like he likes new things. So, I think I'm going to make a call tomorrow morning after breakfast."

"I think that's an amazing and awesome idea. I

believe you two would work well together. I mean, well, I don't know him personally, but he seems—if you see him on TV or hear people talk about him—he seems like a nice person. And you need a nice person."

Lisa nodded just as someone from the kitchen called her name. "Okay then, we have a plan. I guess I need to get in there and cook something right now, and then tomorrow get this hire done."

Alice stood and walked over and hugged her. "Now we know you are going to have some really good help. I'm telling you, girl, this restaurant with you behind it is just going to set records."

"Don't forget you and the inn are going to do the same thing."

They smiled at each other and then walked out of the office feeling overjoyed.

CHAPTER THIRTEEN

Lorna walked out of the house. The baby was sleeping soundly, and she wanted to watch them loading the cows and calves. She wanted to see Dallas. He was now, after all these weeks, working more on the ranch than being in the house taking care of her and Landon. Which was to be expected. He checked on them off and on, but he was busy with the cattle. He still cooked on the grill for them but lately he went to bed by nine because he was up early and knew she was now able to take care of Landon.

But she missed him and wanted to thank him for all he'd done for her, so she was cooking supper for him this evening. And looking forward to it.

He was coming in from the afternoon auction and she wanted him to have a great meal. She knew that he had worked really hard this week on getting these cattle ready for the sale, and she really hoped that he came home happy with the results. She wanted him to know that he was appreciated either way. She walked past the barn and to the large cattle fence. There were two cattle carriers at the gate area. Dallas and the two cowboys he had hired were busy directing the calves through a gate and into the trailer.

Dallas saw her, and he instantly started smiling and came over to the fence.

"I couldn't help coming out before you left. That's a lot of calves."

He smiled, put his elbow close to hers on the fence, and looked closely at her. "It is, just say a prayer, I think you're going to do really well."

"Well, maybe so. If I do, it will be due mostly to you. Because if you weren't here, it wouldn't be happening at all."

He laughed. "I believe God was acting on both our situations when he put us together. Anyway, you watch—we're going to get them loaded and then I'm going to pull out. I should be back here by seven at the latest."

She smiled at him, wanting to—oh, so wanting— to put her arms around him. "Well, dinner will be ready around seven then."

"Are you sure you want to do that? I could pick us up something tonight if you don't feel like cooking."

"I'm absolutely sure. My energy is back, and I want to pay you back for what you're doing."

"Okay, but it's not paying me back—it's giving me a treat."

"Then I'm going to make sure I give you a really good treat. I'm actually a fairly good cook at certain things, so we shall see."

He put his hand on her arm. "All right then, I'm going to go get busy. And I'm looking forward to seeing you when I get home."

"Go for it. See you soon."

He squeezed her arm then walked back and herded the last of the cattle over the next little bit.

When they climbed into the trucks and pulled out, she waved. To be honest, she couldn't care less whether the cattle did good at the sale or not. She was looking forward to Dallas returning. She was looking forward to spending the evening with him.

* * *

Dallas drove home from the cattle sale. He had let the two hired hands each drive a truck with a cattle hauler, and he drove his truck. If Lorna had needed him, he needed to get to her fast. He hadn't been needed but he was eager to get home and see her. He realized that he had called her place home as if it were his home. He had reached a point of thinking of home being where she was. He was in so much trouble—he was letting his heart get out of hand.

He tried pushing the heart thoughts out of his brain and focused on being her friend. He had been pleased to see her bring in a good paycheck for her sale. And he was eager to give it to her.

Then again, he had to be careful because she was cooking supper for him and he had been seeing in her expressions that she had feelings for him also.

Pulling into the drive, he parked his truck next to the garage and jumped out. He walked around to the side and opened the door into the kitchen. "Hello. Is it okay to come in?" He spotted her near the stove as she spun toward him, smiling. His heart did aerobics. He was in trouble and he knew it. He told himself to calm down as he entered.

"You're back." She rushed over and threw her arms around him. "I'm glad to see you." She backed up, as if realizing what she'd done. "So, are you happy?"

He'd hugged her but had to fight off the want to hold onto her forever. "I was happy. This is for you." He tugged the check from his pocket and held it out to her.

Lorna opened it up and her face turned shocked. Her wide eyes met his. "Why so much?"

"Because those cattle are from very good stock and people around here want them."

"Wow. Thank you for doing that. I'm in shock." She put the check over at the end of the counter and then came back. She picked up the spoon she had been using and stirred what looked like ground meat and cut-up bell pepper that he'd bought at the grocery store, along with onions.

He leaned against the corner of the counter. "That looks delicious."

She smiled at him. "It's really not that hard to make but it tastes really good. Honestly, I haven't made it in a long time. My mother loved to make it and taught me. So, I thought we would have it tonight."

"I'm all for it." He realized he hadn't washed his hands since he came in, so he turned and walked to the sink. He turned it on and got busy.

"So was it a big auction?"

"Yes, it was. This is a big cattle and horse area, so the sales are pretty good sized. And obviously, as you saw, profitable."

"So I learned. Thank you so much for doing that. You're very good at what you do, and I'm very grateful you're here."

He dried his hands and then moved back to where he was. She was through stirring the dish and smiled at him. "So is the baby ready to start getting out?"

"Yes. Which means I am too. So, I could go to the grocery store."

"Yes, you could, if you want to. But I was asking because I know you wanted to see my mom's place, and I know she would love for you to visit and to show you around. Then we could eat dinner at Star Gazer Inn."

Her eyes widened. "I would love that. I really would love that. I've been wanting to see it ever since she came to see me. And I've been wanting to see her again too."

"All right then, you tell me what night is good and we'll do it. Since I got these cattle rounded up and sold today, my afternoons are going to be free for a little while. I'm not going to be working late gathering up cattle or anything like that. Although the guys are off for the next couple of days, and I'll be getting your yard mowed again."

"Tomorrow or the next day is good for me. You know I have no plans."

He chuckled. "Then how about tomorrow? If we wake up and it's a pretty day. If, for some crazy reason, we wake up and it's raining, we'll wait until the day it's not raining because you'll want to enjoy her garden area. Does that sound good?"

"It sounds good. But I hope tomorrow's beautiful—as a matter of fact, I believe when I saw the

Weather Channel this morning when I was watching a little television, that it's supposed to be pretty this whole week."

"Well then, that sounds perfect. Now, what do I need to do to help you get ready for this amazing dinner we're getting ready to have?"

"Well, I already put the plates on the table, and I just fed the baby and he's sleeping. So you can grab that glove there and take the rolls out of the oven."

She stepped back as he grabbed the oven mitt and pulled it over his hand, then opened the door and pulled out some beautiful, really beautiful rolls. He set them on the metal counter protector and closed the door to the oven.

She smiled widely. "Oh, they turned out great."

"And they are gorgeous. Where did you get those?"

"I made them. I've always made my own rolls."

He leaned his head to the side and looked at her. "Wow, I cannot wait to eat that. I'm glad you made a lot of them."

"Well, if you'll put them in that red bowl there with the napkins in it and take them into the dining room, I'll get this off the stove. Then we need to grab this vegetable casserole there on the counter."

"I'll bring that."

They worked together and soon had the meal

sitting on the table. It was a meat and vegetable dish and a really nice corn casserole. And the amazing-looking rolls. They sat down and he said a prayer, a thank-you for the food and for her and Landon doing so well. And for the sale of the animals.

They ate and talked, not just about things that had happened but for what she could do with the ranch.

The food was delicious and when they finished, as much as he told himself to thank her and go to his room near the garage, he didn't. "It's nice out there—do you want to go sit and keep talking for a little while?"

Delight filled her face. "I would love to."

And so, they took all the food off the table, put foil on it, put it into the refrigerator, and then quickly scrubbed the plates and put them in the dishwasher and headed outside. This had been a great day. And he was hoping he wasn't about to mess it up. He still had to be careful.

CHAPTER FOURTEEN

It was a beautiful night. The moon was high and bright and lit up the pastures. Lorna sat down in the swing with its padded cushion and room for someone else. Being brave, she patted the cushion beside her and looked at Dallas, and smiled. To her delight, he sat down beside her.

She tried to calm the nerves inside her that were jumping and the desire to take his hand. To lean into him and feel his arm around her shoulders and to kiss him. Oh goodness, she couldn't help it and she leaned slightly his way. His eyes were troubled, and she could see his brain working against him, working against their attraction. Because there was no doubt in her mind that he was attracted to her. But it was clear that he wasn't wanting to step across the line.

"I'm enjoying this evening," he said.

She smiled at him. "I am too. I was really looking forward to being with you, just you and me out here in this beautiful moonlight. Dallas, I am…I know, I shouldn't but I want—"

He leaned in and kissed her. As if he had been waiting. As though he couldn't resist any longer. She couldn't. His kiss was so wonderful, and his arms went around her, pulling her close as he deepened the kiss. Her heart thundered, and she could feel his doing the same thing.

He pulled back and propped his forehead against hers. Both of them were breathing heavily.

"I didn't have the ability to stop myself," he said gently.

She pulled her head back and smiled at him. "And I am so grateful. I've been wanting to kiss you for so long."

He looked thoughtful. "And I have felt the same way for you. But I don't know what we're going to do about this. I work for you."

"No you don't—you help me."

His face looked uncertain. "Yes, but I still have a responsibility to you, and if we start mixing our emotions, what will that mean?"

What did he mean? "It would just mean that we have feelings for each other. I am so happy that you kissed me. And that you told me how you feel. But I can see you are worried, so we can just move slowly. You are helping me—I'm not requiring you to kiss me. I just want you to."

He smiled as he cupped her cheek. "I know that. So, we're going to go slow and get this figured out, okay?"

She leaned her head toward his. "Okay."

And then she kissed him. Her entire life had just taken a step upward.

* * *

It was a beautiful day on Monday and although Dallas was a little uncertain about what he was doing letting his feelings show, he was completely overjoyed by Lorna's kissing him last night. Hopefully he wasn't making a mistake by letting her see how he felt.

She seemed overjoyed by it as he parked the truck at his mother's B&B. He glanced over at Lorna. She looked amazing. She had pulled out a really nice pair of slacks and a pretty blouse with flowers on it and had told him she hadn't worn that in a long time because she hadn't dressed up. It looked great on her, though, and he'd told her so earlier when she was getting in the truck.

Now, she smiled as she looked at the B&B. "It's beautiful."

"Yes, it is. I hope you have a wonderful night. My mom and Lisa are really looking forward to seeing you again."

"And I'm really looking forward to seeing them too. And the restaurant and the B&B. It's amazing even from here. I can't imagine how good the inside looks."

"It's beautiful. It's very beachy."

She rubbed her hands together. "Then let's go."

He laughed and climbed out and opened the back door to get the baby out. He would have liked to have gone around there and helped her out, but he had a sweet baby boy waiting on him. Landon stared up at him as he unbuckled him and then pulled his carrier out. "Hey kiddo, we're about to have a good night." He rubbed his head, making him smile.

Lorna met him at the front of the truck, and they walked to the front door and went inside. His mom stood behind the booking desk.

Her face immediately lit up and she rushed around the counter. "Dallas, you brought her. Oh, Lorna, it's so great to see you." Alice hugged Lorna and then pulled back, holding Lorna's arms. "You look amazing."

"Thank you. Believe me, losing my weight had nothing to do with me. It was all that sweet little boy right there as he had his meals every day. I've actually lost a little bit more than I need to, so I'm trying to eat more and I'm starting to exercise to build my muscles back up a bit."

"Well, you are doing a great job. I'm so glad y'all came." She released Lorna and hugged Dallas but was careful because he was holding the baby carrier with his good arm. She bent over and tickled the baby's chin. "You sweet boy, I am so glad you came to see me tonight." She watched him smile and his eyes grew with excitement. "He is adorable."

"Thank you. I think so too," Lorna agreed.

"Me too," Dallas said. "Did we get here at the right time?"

"Perfect time. Hang on, let me get my helper over here to take my place." She walked around the corner and then she came back, smiling, as a young woman came to take her place at the counter.

She smiled at them. "Y'all have a good time."

They both said they would and then they went down the hallway with his mom. Instead of going straight into the restaurant, she took them up the stairs to show it to Lorna. "Now, several of the rooms are full but I have two that are vacant, so I'm going to show those to you."

"Oh, that's wonderful. This is so pretty. And the paintings on the wall are just beautiful."

His mom reached a door and unlocked it. "Thank

you. We worked hard on it. Seth did amazing work. He was here when you were having the baby. The tall, older man."

"Oh, I remember seeing him when they were carrying me and Landon out. He congratulated me."

"Yes, he did. He's very talented. So here you go, take a look. This room is named Pelican and the decorations, I think, are beautiful."

"Oh my goodness. I bet people who rent this never want to leave." Lorna's expression was amazed as she took in the room.

Dallas studied the room. It was beautiful. It had pale-blue walls and the bed had a lovely cream-colored covering. The window had brightly colored curtains and a beautiful view of the beach. It overlooked the garden and out to the ocean, just like most of the rooms did. The view was amazing this evening: the sun was still in the sky, but probably only had another hour before it lowered.

They went and looked at a second room. It was just as beautiful. The walls were a soft teal color and the curtains were the same as the other room because they had multiple colors in them and fit both colors. His mom had chosen that particular curtain material and then painted each of the rooms one of the tones so that it was something that connected the rooms.

When they headed back downstairs, she led them

into the living room. It was a comfortable, very beachy room and had a unique, colorful couch that sat beneath a painting on the wall.

"That's a beautiful painting," Lorna said, totally focused on the large beach painting.

He knew who had done it, and it was beautiful.

"Thank you. That was painted by Nina, Jackson's fiancée. You haven't met her yet, and we are going to have to fix that. She's been really busy because she's been getting back to doing art shows at galleries. She and my son Jackson are trying to figure out when they can get married. She's been painting in between shows and taking care of her Goldendoodle, Buttercup—oh, he is so cute. Anyway, her life is full right now, but you will meet her because she is thrilled that you had your baby and that Dallas rescued you."

"She sounds very nice. I'll look forward to meeting her. I'm really taken aback by knowing someone I absolutely don't know is thinking about me like that."

Dallas smiled. "You will like her when you meet her. I was going to mention that now that you're starting to get out more, we'll do a few things. And one of the things I was thinking would be good for you was to drive out to my family ranch and let you see it. And meet my brothers too. Who knows—Nina might even be out there."

"That would be great. I have to say, I'm curious about where you were raised, and it just sounds very interesting."

He caught his mom's really bright eyes and the smile that took over her face. He looked back at Lorna. "All right, we'll do it."

"All right, that sounds like a great plan," his mother said. It had been obvious she had been happy about his and Lorna's plans. "Let's go outside so y'all can see the gardens and the beautiful gazebo that Seth built for me. It's for weddings and gatherings. We actually have been scheduling weddings. I have been very surprised at how quickly we have been getting offers and requests and bookings."

He did not miss the hint in his mom's voice. And it made him happy to realize that she was actually rooting for him in a large way. He'd thought about asking her if he was messing up, but her attitude right now clearly said she was hoping he wouldn't waver. He didn't want to waver.

After they looked at the garden area, which was large, his mom led them to the back porch, then over to the outdoor eating area and the table that had been reserved for them. It was at the corner of the outdoor dining area, and had a great view of the garden and the beach.

"Here you two go. Now y'all have a wonderful

meal. I loved showing you two around and now I'll go to the kitchen and let Lisa know you're here so she can come out when she has a free moment to say hello."

"Okay, I'd like Lorna to meet her. But you were supposed to join us." Dallas saw the sparkle in her eyes.

"Yes, we would love for you to join us," Lorna said.

"I'm sorry, I have to work. I just took off enough time to show you around. You call me and come out for lunch one day with me. Tonight, you and Dallas enjoy yourselves." And with a big smile, she turned and left them.

Dallas looked at Lorna and was actually grateful to his mom for giving them this time. He set the baby carrier in the wooden stand that was already waiting on them. Then he pulled out the chair beside it for Lorna. And he sat in the chair right across from her. This was going to be a lovely night.

CHAPTER FIFTEEN

The day after Dallas had brought Lorna to the restaurant and she went out and met her and liked her, Lisa was hoping the two would end up a couple. Now she stood in the kitchen and watched as Zane made one of her dishes.

He looked at her as he flipped the filet mignon over and added the flavoring she preferred. "What do you think—did I add what I was supposed to, or do I need to add more flavorings?"

She studied him. He was being very student-like. He was an unbelievably talented chef, one she could have taken classes from. Just like he was taking a class from her. "It looks like that was probably perfect. But since it's all in that particular container there and, like I told you…just cover that meat up with it and let it cook, I have a feeling that you've done nothing but perfection. I'm very aware of how talented you are."

He shrugged. "I have my talents, just like you do, but I can always learn, and this is all about your recipes. It's not about me at all. I'm just here, being a second to you."

She had been that many times as she had traveled and taken classes and worked one-on-one with great chefs all over the place. Even when she had been married, she had traveled and taken classes. "I understand." She appreciated his attitude.

He lifted the steak from the grill, placed it on a plate, and handed it to her. They walked down to the table at the end of the room and she set the plate on a table, and then she sliced the steak. She handed him a fork and she took a fork from the napkin she'd placed here for them, and she took a bite. It was delicious. It was scary delicious. She had known he was talented. She had given him the recipe and told him how she did it and then he had taken it on.

"This is perfect."

He took a bite, chewed, then swallowed. "I have to say it is. You have created a great combination there."

She realized that compliments from him thrilled her. It wasn't as if he was just someone who had come there to get a great meal from her; he was an outstanding chef himself who had come there to work for her. Eating his offering of her steak was mind-blowing. There was one thing she believed in—and that was giving credit where credit was due.

"When I hired you, I felt really strongly about it. You are very talented. You're probably more talented than I am—"

"I wouldn't say that it's a—"

"I know it's just what someone thinks, but I hired you because out of everybody who came in for an interview, I just couldn't get your abilities off my mind. Or the fact that you wanted to give up your restaurant to come here. And now I'm very, very glad I hired you because this is amazing. And I can only hope that mine tastes somewhat like it."

He chuckled. "Yes, we had yours earlier and you know as well as I do it was better."

"Thank you, but I'm not certain about that. So, I guess tonight we'll work beside each other and then go from there. Get used to each other, and I'll get comfortable with you making the different dishes."

He smiled at her. "Sounds great. And I have to tell you once again I'm thrilled to be here. I'm actually looking for a home on Star Gazer Island because I really like this area. I don't want to drive all the way back into the city. I'm ready for something more laid-back. And I want to be closer so it will be quicker to get here. So if some sort of craziness happens and it's not my day to work but you need me, all you have to do is call."

Her insides reacted to his words and she was once again startled by her reactions to him. "I think that's a very good idea." As far as work was concerned—but these tingling reactions needed to go away. She was not attracted to him. She wasn't. Nope, she just admired his talent.

* * *

"Okay, this is my question," Nina said as she and Alice and Buttercup walked along the beach. It was two o'clock in the afternoon and she had called Alice and asked her whether she would have time to take a little walk with her.

Alice had been thrilled and ready.

"So, I looked at our schedules and I contacted all of the family and as it turned out, everyone has the weekend open four weeks away. So, I think that we are going to get married on that weekend. I can work hard to get the garden decorated, and put the invitations out, and if anyone can come, they can come. If not, as long as family is there, then that's what is most important to us. The important question is, would you be able to take off that weekend—I mean, at least that Saturday afternoon?"

Alice threw her arms around her and hugged her tight. "I would take off whenever to be at your and Jackson's wedding. I think that will be a great weekend and I can help you as much as you need it."

"Hallelujah! I was hoping you could. And I would love your help decorating, but only if you have time that week before the wedding."

"I wouldn't miss it. I would love to offer for the restaurant to cook for you but at this point there is no way I can ask Lisa to cook an extra meal for a group. Who would we get to cook for it? I know you already have someone in line for everything."

They were walking again along the beautiful beach. "I've called a really good florist in town and she's been in wholeheartedly. And then Reba from Reba's Wedding Delights is in for the meal and the wedding cake. Her business does great."

"You're amazing. I'm impressed and so excited."

"I'm so excited I can hardly believe it," Nina said. "And your son will be, too, when I break this to him. He will be so thrilled."

"But do you know he has that Saturday free?"

Nina laughed. "Yes, he does. And believe me, he has already told me he will drop anything I need him to in order to marry me, but I don't want him to drop something. I want him to just come and have a good time, and I just want it to work out for both of us.

Anyway, when I leave you, I'll go tell him and we'll celebrate. I'll quickly work up some plans and then I'll let you know. I've questioned everyone in the family and they're all excited. I just knew that you had a new business and you're working most weekends, but you've made my day. Now hopefully Seth will get to come. I haven't asked him but since I know he doesn't work on Saturday, it's more than likely he can."

"I'll ask him tonight. Actually, I have a date with him. Since I work most days, I take off one and we eat out and spend time together."

"Well, let's talk a minute about Seth. I think he's absolutely amazing. Are y'all just friends or have you actually moved into the one-on-one? I mean, it looks like that but I don't want to assume something."

Alice chuckled. "We have actually moved into being a couple. Well, we haven't moved deeply. I've actually only kissed him a few times."

"I am thrilled. Maybe tonight you can up the kissing part."

"Maybe. You know, it was a little bit strange at first, going from being a widow and opening a restaurant and adjusting to a life that's so much different from what I had when William was alive. But honestly, I'm adjusting and Seth has helped me. I mean, he's gone through it, too, but he's had longer, so he hasn't pressured me at all. He's an amazing guy.

And I'm so very blessed that he came into my life."

"I am too. And I'm wondering…do you think you'll marry him?"

Alice's insides trembled. "Maybe. I mean, I would like to but we're going to date longer. I would have to get adjusted to the idea of remarrying and not just because of losing my first love but because I just can't imagine going through that again. So I have to get used to that."

"I can see that would be hard. But from what I'm seeing as you two move into this relationship, things seem to come naturally. You know what I mean?"

"Yes, I do. Anyway, enough about me. I think that we need to head back so you can go find my son and give him this good news. I cannot wait for him to know."

Nina smiled. "Well, honestly, I can't agree more, so let's turn around and head back. You have made our day."

CHAPTER SIXTEEN

Seth was having a great evening. He had picked Alice up and they had gone on a short boat ride and then he had surprised her by taking her to his house. He had fixed the meal tonight. And she had yet to see his house. As the boat moved across the water toward it, her mouth fell open.

"That's your house? It's so pretty. I mean, wow."

"I'm glad you like it. I saw it and immediately liked the way it looked." He pulled the boat up to the dock and then tied it off. After a moment, he had them walking to the back patio and he opened the double doors that led into the house. He let her enter into the living area and kitchen space.

"It's not humungous, but it's just me. It's very comfortable and there's room for a party if I wanted to throw one. Two bedrooms, and then this big living space and a nice kitchen."

She turned toward him. "I love your decorating, too. And something in here smells wonderful."

"Well, good. I've made a stuffed flounder."

"I can't wait."

"I'm glad. Hopefully since I've been letting it just stay warm, it hasn't totally overcooked. But it's been on a very low temperature."

"I'm sure it's perfect."

Within minutes, they had washed their hands and carried the food dishes out onto the table on the patio. He lit the three candles, and then they sat down as the sun settled on the horizon. He had cooked a simple meal with the fish and then baked potatoes and rolls. He liked to cook but he didn't go overboard.

They ate and talked about the business and then about the wedding that was now coming up. He was very glad that he had the date open because he was glad to be able to take Alice. "I'm very happy for those two. From what I understand, with his schedule and her schedule, it was going to be awhile, so to find a spot open that quick is a great thing."

"Yes, it is. I'm not sure what's going to happen when she moves out of the house next door. I'm not sure if she's going to rent it or sell it, but I'll have a new neighbor next door."

"Well now, this is just from my thoughts, but have

you thought about maybe you renting it or buying it so that you're not living in the inn all the time?"

"Oh no, I haven't thought about that. Hmm, I don't know. Umm, no, that wouldn't work for me...I need to be in what I have."

He liked to hear that actually because one day he hoped she'd move in with him. So the fact that she wasn't thinking about putting money into a place for just her pleased him. Reassured him.

"I'm sure it will work out."

"I am too."

"So tell me about your new chef at the inn."

"I think it's going to be great. He's a wonderful chef. You know, he's run that other restaurant for several years and it has a great reputation. And he's a nice guy, from what I know. I mean, you can read about him sometimes in the magazines. He's been around long enough and his name is popular enough that he's actually made the magazines some. But from what I can tell, he's a very nice person and he wanted to work for Lisa. So that tells me he's a very smart person and from what she told me, he's moving out here to Star Gazer Island. He's tired of living in Corpus. I think he lives close to the business and he was probably just ready for something different. And you and I both know there's not much of a place that would be better than here. I love this area."

"I do too. I mean, after Jen had died, it didn't take me long to move out of the city and come here. This is where I came to recoup and I couldn't leave. I didn't need that big job anymore and I always liked repairing things and building things because it helped me mentally, emotionally—and of course, my boat…spending time out there on that water. It was basically God's medicine. I couldn't pass it up—couldn't leave it. So yeah, I understand him."

"I don't know if he's had anything, you know, real emotional or hard in his life, so I don't know if that could be part of it. But from what it sounds like, he's just ready for something good."

"That's okay too. And, you know, I don't really know him. I do know that that restaurant is very popular, but she needed some help. I knew going into this there was no way that talented woman would be able to hold that restaurant down for long by herself. So I was actually expecting her to hire someone right off at the beginning, you know."

"I did, too. But I think she wanted to get it like she wanted it before she hired someone else—you know, get the rhythm down and get all her recipes perfected. She's really overworked and of course she is very tired and hasn't gotten to rest a lot. I know that I'm not there tonight but he's working and she's watching him and teaching him her ways and I'm thrilled."

"I am too. I have to tell you, the inn is a great

place and it's the talk of the town. Honestly, I noticed that all kinds of people come at lunch, and then dinner. All I can say right now is that I'm glad you're not there. I'm glad that you're at dinner at my place and enjoying my dish for you."

She smiled at him. "And I am too."

And then, to his surprise, she leaned forward from her chair at the corner of the table, and she cupped his face, then let her hand slide behind his neck and she pulled him to her and she kissed him.

She kissed him—oh yeah, he was ecstatic.

* * *

She was kissing him. She had planned it, but now she was shaking as his arms went around her and they leaned from chair to chair and kind of lost it.

Finally, he pulled back and smiled. "I am a very delighted man right now. I have been dreaming of a kiss like that from you."

"Well, it's taken me a little while to give myself permission to move forward like that. I mean, I'm moving forward but to give in to what I feel right now was a pretty substantial feeling."

He cupped her face. "And how do you feel?"

"Absolutely wonderful. I hope you do, too."

"Oh yeah, I do. Are you through eating?"

"Yes, there's really nothing left for me to eat on that plate."

He smiled, stood, and took her hands and helped her to her feet. He walked her over to a swing at the edge of the porch; they sat and they looked out at the ocean.

"I'm very glad you came into my life," Alice said.

He held her hand and gave it a gentle squeeze. "I'm the same way. I never dreamed that me opening a new business would lead me to you, to love."

She stared into his eyes, which were very emotional as he said the words. She nodded. "I agree. I do love you, Seth. And I'm grateful that God led us to each other."

She couldn't get over that part. When God took William, she was devastated and it took her almost two years to realize that she needed a new life. To know that opening this inn was what she wanted. But finding a new love? No, she never even suspected that. "So I guess we're on our way to getting a life started."

"It looks that way. But don't feel obligated to me just because we've let our feelings out. You have a lot on your plate right now and I understand that."

"That sounds like a good plan right now. I'm so glad to have our relationship on open ground now."

He pulled her close. His eyes were beautiful as they bore into hers and sent her heart tingling and every nerve in her body reacting.

"I'm just a very blessed and happy man right now." And then he kissed her.

CHAPTER SEVENTEEN

Dallas had loaded Lorna into the truck and the sweet sleeping baby also, and they were headed toward his family's place, the McIntyre Ranch.

"So, I'm going to meet some of your brothers?" Lorna asked.

He smiled at her. "Yes. I know you're going to meet my oldest brother, Jackson, who is the top runner of the ranch—he's marrying Nina. I was hoping she would be here for you to meet, but she had a business appointment. But my two other brothers, Riley and Tucker, will be there also."

"Okay. I look forward to meeting them. And y'all have a gigantic ranch, right?"

"Pretty much. It's got a long history with my family. We've been at it our whole life but Daddy and his dad and granddaddy have been building it for generations. Daddy really brought it into a huge business, though. Jackson is the president of the business now and he's got that attitude where he really likes dealing with people and it works. He's very much like our dad. Now Tucker, he likes the business of working a ranch, so he's basically over what's going on and he loves it.

"Then, I like rodeoing, so as you can see, I'm not involved. But I like ranching and I have to tell you since I've been at your smaller ranch, I have really enjoyed myself. And then we have just all enjoyed the life of freedom that we have. But then there's Riley." He grinned at her.

"Riley likes being on the ranch but he's a very creative guy. And he's actually looking to start a campground. We have a very nice stretch of oceanfront property and I'm very intrigued by what he's doing, even though I haven't really talked to him much about it. I have a really strong feeling he's going to go through with it. I mean, honestly, it would be neat to have something like that. People would come out and enjoy the area. Groups is what I think he's looking at. You know, having like a group of campers who want to come out and have a special time. And one of the groups he's focusing on or, I can say, the main group he is focusing on is women campers."

"Your family sounds great. And Riley sounds

intriguing. There's a lot of single women out there who like to do things and as a single woman, it's not as easy to load up and do something you would normally enjoy doing. They come up with these groups of women who do things together, so I bet there are women camping groups out there who would love to do that."

He glanced from the road and looked over at her again. "You are exactly on target. That's what he thinks. He was on his way home one day and he stopped to get gas and he met this woman who was pulling a little tiny trailer, and they talked for a minute, and I think he liked her a lot. She didn't tell him her name before she got in her vehicle and drove off. But she had told him about where she'd been, told him about the camp and the group she camped with that weekend. It got him to thinking and he hasn't stopped thinking about it since meeting her. Honestly, I haven't personally figured out if it's her or the camping that has drawn him toward it, but no matter…it's interesting."

"It really is. It will be fun watching it and seeing what happens."

"I think so too. Anyway, now you know about my brothers."

They pulled into the drive, and she saw the gate to the ranch and smiled.

"It's kind of cute, isn't it? Well, my dad would

have gotten mad if you said cute, but that's what my mom always called it."

"Yes, it is, and professional."

"Yup, I think so too. So here we go."

They drove up the long lane to the ranch house and then he parked the truck. Before they got out, his brothers had come out of the barn and the house. They all walked over to the truck as he was getting the baby out.

"Hey guys, we're here and I'd like to introduce you to Lorna and Landon."

"Hello, I'm Jackson, and we are really glad to meet you. Glad my brother has been able to help you and that you and the baby are doing well."

"And I'm Tucker. It's very nice to meet you and the baby. We're glad y'all made it through that ordeal. We're glad that Dallas was home and heard you and found you."

"Me too."

"And I'm Riley, and I'm really glad that you're okay and that that cute baby is also. It was a hard but rewarding day. And you know, one day, it might turn out to be more." His gaze went from Dallas back to Lorna. "Who knows? Something else could happen out of the encounter. I know for sure that he's gotten healthier with his shoulder. I think it's almost well, so that's a good thing. You blessed him because if he'd been out here on the ranch, he would have been bored stiff. He wouldn't have had a distraction like taking care of you and the baby and getting your ranch handled."

Lorna smiled. "Well, you're right. I am so blessed to have him in my life. I still can't even imagine how it happened. I mean, when I went into labor out there on the beach, there was no one around so in my mind, my life was just about to be destroyed, and then there he came. It was like a blessing jogging across the sand. And I'm going to forever be grateful."

All of his brothers smiled at her. And she smiled back. She had the strangest feeling that every one of them were maybe hoping that she and Dallas would get together. And she absolutely liked that idea.

* * *

After Lorna met all of his family, he drove around the ranch and let her see a portion of it. There was no way that in a visit or a day you could see all of the thousands of acres that belonged to their ranch. But he wanted her to see where he'd come from because she was curious, so he took her to view a couple of the places he had really enjoyed as a kid. Took her to see the portion of the river they had swam in growing up and it still made a very neat place to visit. It was a

147

beautiful area. She loved it. Then he drove her to see how the ranch had some high hill sections that overlooked much of the other parts of the ranch. They were sitting there now. It was gorgeous.

"This is really stunning at sunset," he said. "There's just so much to admire and see. And the clouds, if they're out, they make the sky look amazing. And then all that flowing pasture and being able to see the river running through it and the cattle…it was just one of my favorite places."

"I love it. Look how huge it is."

He chuckled. "Yes, it is. One thing I learned as I grew up on this ranch is it's huge. It's got around two hundred thousand acres, and in Texas now, there are so many ranches that have far more acreage than that. But compared to most, this place is big."

"Huge." She chuckled.

"You know, this place has its beauty—it has its special spots—but so does your place. That's a pretty twenty thousand acres. And it holds a really good amount of cattle."

"You're right. I know that it's good from listening to you tell me." She smiled.

"Yeah, I know I tell you that a little too much but it's the truth. I love your place."

She touched his hand. "And I'm very glad."

He smiled, backed the truck out, and headed back toward the ranch area. When they pulled into the barn area, he turned off the truck and then they got out. He got Landon and they went into the barn.

"This is where we've always put our horses with new colts. We have two colts now. They are around five weeks old, I think." He led her down the way to where there were two stalls and two colts.

"They're so adorable. I wonder if any of the horses that I have are going to have colts?"

"I don't know, but I have a feeling that there's about three of them that are. I'm going to go through the paperwork and see if I can locate their dates. I'm sure he's got them in there. And then we will figure out what you want to do with some of the colts that are out there since he has them at several ages. If you want to sell them, we can, but if you want them to get two years old and then sell them, maybe we can train them, make sure they're customer-friendly and not just little wild animals. They'd sell for more."

She looked at him. "You know I have no idea how to train a horse, so if we committed to doing that, it would be on you."

His eyes twinkled. "Yes, ma'am, it would."

She grinned. "Then I'm all for that."

"And that being the case, I was thinking my oldest

brother is getting married in about four weeks. And I'm wondering if you and that little one there might want to go with me to the wedding?"

"Oh, that would be lovely. I'd be thrilled to go with you. I'm thinking it's a wonderful invitation."

And then, eyes sparkling, she leaned in and kissed him, and he had to agree with her; it had been a good idea, as far as he was concerned. It was an amazing idea.

CHAPTER EIGHTEEN

"I am so glad you had such a wonderful time." Alice smiled at the couple, the Stewards. They had come in for four days and had thoroughly enjoyed being at the Star Gazer Inn. They had walked the beach; they had enjoyed lunch, dinner, and breakfast most of the time, other times trying out a couple of other local restaurants but always coming back for Lisa's cooking. They had also loved the gardens and she had spotted them several times sitting on one of the benches, enjoying each other and watching the sunset.

After they had left, hand in hand, she smiled. She loved watching everyone enjoy each other. She loved feeling as if she were helping someone get to know their partner better or enjoy life better. There was nothing about being here at her B&B that she was disappointed in.

"You sure are smiling." Lisa came out of the dining area.

"I am. I was just thinking about how much I enjoy being here. And how much everyone who comes here enjoys it."

"Yes, they seem to. I know I get a lot of compliments in the kitchen area, and it just makes me so happy."

She studied her best friend. "So, tell me, how is your new chef doing?"

Lisa took a deep breath and her eyebrows scrunched. "He's really good, great, and all the workers enjoy him. And I'm really startled at how he just takes my instructions. You know he's a very, very respected chef, so it is really startling. And a lot of the people who have been coming in to eat have been overjoyed when they realized he was cooking. Not everyone sees him in the back but some do and it's actually a little bit nerve-racking to me how excited they get."

"Are you jealous?"

"Well, I could be, but no, actually, I'm not. Because they tell me that they really like what we're cooking here and that it's great that he's here helping me because he is so talented. So the majority of them are actually giving me compliments, which sounds horrible to say that. But I guess, honestly, I worked really hard to get this far and I'm enjoying the compliments. It's really something I needed."

Alice wrapped her arm around her friend's waist and gave her a side hug. "It's very well deserved and I think you did right, hiring him. I think in the long run you two will make a great team."

"I hope you're right. I think you're right. And actually, right now since breakfast is over, I'm heading home for a little while in the middle of the day. I'm not just heading into the little rest area you have set up for me outside your office. Because of him, I'm getting to go home."

Alice laughed. "Well, I'm thrilled. So you're getting to skip lunch?"

"I am. I'm going to go home and I'm going to enjoy five hours before I come back at four o'clock."

"Well, good. That's what you're supposed to do. All right then, you get going. You don't want to waste that time."

"No, I really don't. He told me to relax, that he would make sure lunch was like I would do it and then we would give him some more lessons at dinner tonight so that soon he would be able to do dinner for me when I wanted the evening off."

"Well, that sounds intriguing, so I think he's the perfect guy. Now, go relax, enjoy, and let the guy you hired take care of things."

She watched her friend head out the front door. Normally she came and went through the side door that came into the kitchen and she still did. Before they opened, that was usually where Alice was. But now that the kitchen was actually open and busy and the front desk needed Alice, Lisa had come to the front area to see her. They were both busy and happy. Alice was thrilled for her friend; she deserved this new chef. And he sounded very determined to make this work. That pleased Alice greatly.

* * *

Nina took her dog on a walk early. It was two weeks before her wedding and she was so excited. The first week that they had decided to do the wedding, she and Alice had worked on getting invitations out to people. They had limited it some and were expecting at least two hundred people. She wasn't from here originally, so she didn't know how many people from her hometown would show up. But she wanted to invite them anyway, just in case they wanted to come.

Today she was going back up to the wedding shop and trying on her dress. It fit her snugly then flowed around her knees. It was armless, with a V-neck. It wasn't over-the-top fancy; it wasn't amazing like so many of the wedding dresses that she had seen and admired were, but for her it worked. She loved it. But it had to have been taken up a little bit in the breast area because she wasn't as big as the dress had been made for, and it had to be taken up a little in the waist. She was still so excited to try it on today.

She was almost back to the gate to her house when she spotted Alice and Lorna. She had only met Lorna one time, so she turned and headed over just as they spotted her. "Are y'all going for a walk? It's a great morning for it."

"Yes, we are." Alice gave her a hug. "It's so good to see you and let you see Lorna again. We were just talking about your and Jackson's wedding."

"I'm really excited to get to come. I hope you don't mind that Dallas invited me?"

"No, not at all. I should have already put you on the list. Anybody who is invited to the wedding is always welcome to bring someone with them, but you are officially invited."

Alice touched Nina's arm. "Don't worry about that...I did send her an invitation. Even though she's only met you the one time."

"Well, I'm pretty certain that in the future we will see each other more often than one or two times."

"I hope so," Lorna said and looked like she meant it.

"So what are you girls up to? This little fella is

155

adorable." She reached over and rubbed the baby's belly. "Can I hold him for a minute?"

"Sure you can." Lorna handed him over, and Nina gladly took the cute little baby.

She was so ready to have a baby. She hoped that Jackson would be ready soon too. She was going to ask him. She looked at them. "I am ready to have a baby."

"I don't think my son's going to argue with you too much. You should be able to get what you want as quickly as you want."

"I think so too. Landon is adorable." She handed him back.

"We've gotten everything sent out. We have the food all ordered, and the decorations are all waiting to be put out. So everything is set. I'm going to try on my dress right now. They've done the few alterations I needed done to it so, after that, as hard as it is to believe, we're almost ready."

"Great. It will be wonderful." Her future mother-in-law hugged her again.

"It's going to be beautiful, I can tell," Lorna said. "I'm really looking forward to it, and I can tell you that Dallas is thrilled. He knows you make his brother happy, and that makes him happy."

Nina liked that. "You just made my day. I love Dallas, and I'm so glad he's home and getting healthy. And most of that is due to you coming into his life when you did. And I can't help but ask—and I know it's none of my business—but how are y'all doing?"

She knew she probably shouldn't have asked that, and she saw the slightly shocked expression on Alice's face. But oh well, she couldn't help herself. "I know I'm being a little too personal, maybe."

Lorna bit her lip as if she were thinking. "I'm crazy about him. And he likes me too. He told me he loved me, and I told him I loved him. Therefore, we're in fairly deep, in a really good way. He has helped me so much, and I was so worried as I was falling for him that he would be upset because he was just helping me. Thank goodness, he loves me, but we are moving slow. We don't want to go too fast."

Nina and Alice both reached for her and they hugged her around Landon. Congratulations were given from both of them before they let her go.

"I think it's wonderful," Nina said. "He's a great guy. And I think you are just what he needed, and it sounds like he is just what you needed."

"Exactly," Alice agreed. "I'm a very happy mother, I'll just let you both know. And, Nina, you better go and get done what you need to get done. If there's anything I can do for you, give me a call. And Lorna, let's get on our walk and do a little talking before you have to get this sweet baby back home for a nap."

"Bye! Have fun." Nina smiled as she watched them head down the beach. She turned and walked back to her gate and went inside. "Buttercup, I think something wonderful just happened. I really like that girl, and I really think she's making my sweet, soon-to-be brother-in-law into a very happy man. I'm wondering if we'll be having another wedding soon. I hope so."

* * *

Lorna drove into town and parked on the main street. There were several places for women to shop, and she was hoping that she would find something to wear to the wedding. She had been so thrilled to be asked to the wedding and she wanted to make sure that she looked great. She loved Dallas; he was just so amazing. Every time they spent a second together was an opportunity for her to make sure he understood her feelings and for this event, she knew she wanted a beautiful dress.

She was a little over the top with jealousy, thinking about his brother getting married. And she couldn't help but hope that somewhere along the way that she could be a part of the McIntyre family. She hoped with all of her heart that that would happen, but she couldn't rush him. She could make certain that she looked as good as possible. She got out of the car and then opened the back door and lifted the baby carrier out. Landon had gone to sleep, so she was very careful as she carried him inside, snoozing in his carrier. She walked inside the first women's clothing store, and it was nice.

The young woman came from behind the counter, smiling. "How are you? I'm Carol and I'm here if you need anything. What are you looking for…anything specific?"

"I'm Lorna. And I'm actually looking for something to wear to a wedding."

"Your wedding?"

"No, I'll be a guest. It will be an outdoor wedding on their ranch."

Carol smiled and then cocked her fingers as she headed down the aisle. "I think we might have something that would appeal to you. You did well, picking us. We keep a variety of clothing available for parties, and we even keep some white and cream dresses that are fancy and available in case someone comes into town and suddenly decides to get married. Of course, the cream dresses can be worn as a party dress, not just as a wedding dress."

"That's why when I asked my friend where to go that she suggested this store first. She said it had a lot to choose from." She was grateful Alice seemed like someone who always knew the right thing, and when she saw the rack, just looking at it made her realize that this store had a good bit to choose from.

"So this is a start, anyway. Do you want to set the baby down and kind of dig through there on your own, or do you want to sit over there in that chair and let me bring things to you?"

"I'm fine. I'll just set him down here and I'll take my time and go through them. Where's the dressing room?"

"Right there." She pointed at the room right across from the rack.

"Perfect. I will go through these and I'll pick up some, then I'll take my baby in there and I'll start trying some on."

Carol smiled and looked at Landon. "He's adorable. And it looks like he went to sleep just to help you."

"I tried to come when he would be taking his nap because he would be quieter, and I could focus more on the clothing."

Carol winked at her. "Well, you did a great job. If you need me, you just call me—like if you need a different size, I can get it for you."

"Okay, thank you."

As Carol walked off, Lorna set her baby inside the dressing room where she could see him with the door open but wouldn't have to pick him up and move him. And then she turned and started looking through the dresses. It didn't take long for her to have several dresses in the dressing room. Some were longer, some were mid-thigh; she really didn't know what she wanted but she felt as if she probably wanted something longer.

She went inside the dressing room and when she tried on the third dress, she fell in love. It was actually a light-beige dress that fit her perfectly and hung just above her ankles. When she put a pair of heels on with the dress, it would give it a unique length and look, and she loved it. With a sigh and a smile, she took a deep breath, turned a circle and studied the look, and knew that despite the light color this was her dress. She redressed and carried the dress and her baby back out the door.

"You picked one of my favorite dresses. And that color—I know it looks awesome on you," Carol said.

"And it fits me absolutely perfect. Now if I could just find a pair of shoes to match it—a cream color— I'll be fixed up."

"We don't have shoes but there is a store three doors down that does. I have a feeling you'll find what you need over there." Carol got the dress rung up and in a plastic cover on a hanger, and then handed it to her. "I hope you'll come back and try on our other things. We work hard to try to have something to please everybody."

"And I absolutely believe it. I will be back. I'm just not ready to buy a lot of new clothes since I just had my little fella not too long ago and I need to adjust my weight a bit."

"We'll be here. Our owner has had this shop here for years, so you just come in when you're ready."

She smiled and then headed out the door, thrilled that they had had what she needed. She knew Dallas was going to love it, and that was exactly what she'd hoped when she'd come in search of the perfect dress.

CHAPTER NINETEEN

Dallas had gotten a call from his manager, who was in charge of helping him handle all his sponsors. He was grateful to have their support. For their support, he did television and computer advertisements, and he knew it was time to do some. However, with his shoulder the way it was, he'd had to postpone a lot of his advertisements.

"Dallas, so we've got a couple of ads that have to be done. Are you...is your shoulder repaired enough to where you can come out for a couple days of filming?"

He took a deep breath. He wasn't going to tell them just yet that he was pretty sure he was going to pull out of rodeo. Sometimes you were able to keep sponsors or keep doing advertising after you quit. It depended on the sponsors and what they were looking for. He didn't need the sponsors; he had the family inheritance and he had been able to put his sponsor money aside too, so he was not like a lot of people. He was very blessed, very lucky. But he felt bad leaving them hanging.

"When and where would it be at? I can do it. My shoulder is far better and as long as I watch overdoing it, I can do an ad." Not that it would ever be fully repaired or that riding a bareback bull wouldn't immediately tear it up again.

"I'm glad you're doing better. We were thinking about the end of the week, if you could do it. Over there at the arena on their ranch that was near Fort Worth." This was a large sponsor who had a small ranch they used to test their food enhancer with the cattle they raised. It was about five hours away, not horribly far away, but if it took him two days to film and a day to drive down, it would be four days to get up there and back. *Could he leave here for four days?*

He could have his two hired hands work while he was gone, working the cattle, repairing fences, and that would cause them to be around if Lorna had an emergency. He thought she'd be fine, but he couldn't help worrying. She had been going and getting the groceries, and she'd gone and gotten her dress for Jackson and Nina's upcoming wedding. And then there was the time they spent in the evening in the swing on the porch. He was completely ready to get married and there was no denying it. All he wanted to do was ask her, but so far he hadn't convinced himself to do it.

"I hate to leave responsibility behind, so tell me what day I need to be there, send me the address and I'll show up. At whatever time you tell me."

"I knew you'd come through for me. All right, can you be here Wednesday and let's film Wednesday and Thursday?"

His brain worked, and he couldn't remember anything specific on those days. "Yes, I'll be there. And it's two advertisements?"

"Yes, we're doing one for Jeff Row and his business there at the ranch, and then the dog food company would bring dogs and we'll film theirs on the ranch the next day."

"Sounds like a plan. I'll be there."

They hung up and he let his responsibilities sink in. The responsibilities that mattered to him now were here on Lorna's ranch. He wanted to make this into a great place to carry on Lewis Franks's name. Landon's father. Lewis was worth a lot of money from the equipment part that had made him so much money. Dallas had learned through several different people that he'd loved working with these ranch animals more than anything. The horses and the cattle had a good reputation, and Dallas wanted to make it even better. He was sure that Lewis would be glad to know that somebody was thinking of his ranch and his son. Because Landon was who he was thinking about, wanting to build the ranch up considering Lewis wasn't there to do it. Landon would never know his dad, but he was going to inherit this beautiful place when he grew up. Although Dallas wanted to be his daddy and married to his mother, he had no plans to not let the little kid inherit from his real daddy through knowing who had built this ranch.

Dallas knew he was going to do these two advertisements and then he was going to let them know that he was quitting. Let them know that he could continue representing them if they wanted him to, and if they didn't, he had no problem with it. He was just ready to get on with his life.

* * *

Lorna was rocking Landon in his bedroom the evening after she had bought the beautiful dress. She smiled down at him. He had just finished eating and was now happily going to sleep. His little face was playing with smiles and grins and making her smile as she watched him. Her child was an amazing little fella, and it was going to be fun to watch him grow up. She could tell that Dallas was crazy about him, too. She had hopes, so many hopes of them becoming a family.

There was a tap on the door though the door was open. She knew that Dallas was standing near the wall and not coming in if he suspected that she might be feeding the baby.

"Come in. It's safe," she said, knowing that she hoped one day...well, she was never going to allow herself to have sex before marriage again, even if she loved someone. She just couldn't risk it. Even though she was so ready to call Dallas hers in every way. But though he had been treating her as if they were a committed couple, he had said nothing so far about them moving forward in the future as husband and wife.

He smiled as he came through the door. "How are you today?"

Her heart beat rapidly. "I'm great. This little fella is doing great too. He ate everything he was supposed to and now he's sleeping. He has amazing habits that he just follows perfectly. I think he's probably spoiling me. You know what I mean. I could have a baby one day that is far different from this." She laughed. "But it wouldn't matter—I would love him or her just the same."

Dallas's expression wavered. "I'm quite sure you would be able to handle any baby and I'm pretty sure he's the way he is because you are such an attentive mother."

"Maybe, but maybe not. How's your day going?"

"It's going good, but I have something I have to talk to you about and I didn't know how much longer you would be in here. I can either leave now and go out to the barn and come back later, or I can wait."

What did he want to talk about? She could tell by the sound in his voice that something was bothering him. "I can put him down now. He's completely asleep so he won't mind. Give me a second and I'll be right there."

"Okay, I'll be out here." He turned and left the room.

Feeling suddenly scared, she placed Landon in his crib. *Was Dallas going back to the rodeo?* The idea was like a fist to her stomach. And her heart began to ache. She took a deep breath and then headed toward the living room.

He was standing in front of the fireplace when she got there, and he walked over and immediately took her hands and led her to the couch. They both sat down and he continued to hold her hands.

"Are you going back to the rodeo?" she couldn't help but ask.

He shook his head and his lip curled up just a little. "No, I'm not. I didn't mean to scare you like that. I'm going to resign from the rodeo first of next week. But I am a representative of several products and commercials for them had to be put off while I was injured. My manager contacted me this morning and I need to do a commercial for two of the companies. I do owe them, so I'm leaving tomorrow afternoon for the five-hour trip to a ranch outside of Fort Worth. We start shooting the next morning, on Wednesday, for a commercial on a supplement for horses. And on Thursday we'll do the other product, which is a dog food, using an area on the ranch. It often takes all day to get these done, so I probably won't head home until Friday. I'll leave early."

Her stomach curled and her heart raced. *He had said home.* Of course, this was his hometown—his ranch was just across town—but she thought he meant this ranch. She kept her thoughts to herself. "I understand. We'll be fine."

"The guys are going to come in and feed the animals and make sure everything's fine during the day, and they're supposed to check on you. So if you need anything, they're more than happy to help you. They'll be knocking on your door before they leave each evening to check on you."

"They're both really nice, so I'll take them up on it if I need them. But I won't. I've been feeling amazing and it's not like I have to have a babysitter—which I loved you being my babysitter. I still do. But anyway, you had responsibilities and you still do, so you have to go do what you have to do. And about you retiring next week, I think that's...well, I told you that before...but I think that's a good decision."

He smiled and pulled her into his arms and hugged her. "Okay, we're going to get this done and then when I get back on Saturday, we're going to work the ranch here and get ready for Jackson and Nina's wedding the following Saturday. I have to help out with a couple of days of decorating."

"Okay." She leaned back, looking at him. "Do you need some help? I would love to help if Nina needed me to."

"I'm sure she considered it but she doesn't want to take your time away from the baby."

"I see. Well, if I see her this week, I'm going to still let her know that I would love to help. Or at least come look."

"I'm sure that she would be thrilled for you to come out. I'm going to miss you while I'm gone, you know."

She'd been trying to avoid letting her feelings show and his words sent sparks racing through her...and hope. "Well, I'm going to miss you too. However, I'm going to force myself to survive. And then celebrate when you come back." *There, she was being positive.*

He pulled her into his arms, hugged her tight and

then kissed her, completely turning her insides into noodles.

"I need to go get to work. I will talk to you later at dinner, and then I'll be here half the day tomorrow."

"It's going to be at least four days that I have to do without a kiss from you."

A huge smile grew on his face and his eyes sparkled as he leaned forward. "I can do it again. I definitely don't want you suffering."

And then he kissed her, and she just very nearly fainted.

CHAPTER TWENTY

Lorna needed something to do while Dallas was gone, or she was going to be depressed. She now stood in a huge furniture and decoration store. If she was going to live in that house, she wanted to start making it look more like hers, or at least have some new items. She wasn't one to shop a lot; she had never had a lot of money to shop, but she had it now. She had a new place, a new baby, and a home that nothing in it belonged to her. She wasn't going to get so much that if Dallas decided to marry her that they couldn't add things of his desire too. But today she needed to be busy and make some changes while he was on his work trip.

She saw a beautiful chair that she loved. It was made of a leather material that was soft and when she sat down in it, she was so comfortable. It would replace the chair she sat in now that was fairly worn, even though she was certain it was probably the chair that Lewis sat in most of the time and she should feel guilty getting rid of it. But she wanted a chair to sit in that she had chosen and that wasn't so worn by someone else. So she bought it.

And then she found a couch and a couple of chairs to go with it, and she bought them. And then she found a couple of other things that went well with them. She looked at what she had chosen and knew that she was about to have her own living room. She continued to look around and found a few things for the kitchen that she wanted to replace. Some of the things that Lewis used, like his sugar holder, which was a cow, were not her style. She liked the cream-toned jar with Sugar spelled out across it, so she bought it and the rest of the set.

There were other things she wanted to buy so badly but didn't because she would wait until later...hoping things changed soon. A master bedroom suite was top of the list. She wasn't sleeping in the master bedroom right now. She had chosen not to do that, not yet, and was sleeping in one of the guest rooms next to the baby's room. When she did choose to finally move into the master bedroom, it would be completely redecorated, with a new bed and dressers. She wanted it to be hers and Dallas's. She looked at several different sets and then, because it was making her wish and hope too much, she left the bed area and headed home with Landon.

She reached the Texas Ready Diner and pulled into the parking space, deciding that she and Landon would have dinner here before going home. It was on the way and always busy, so a good place to stop.

She went into the little diner and they were seated at a table next to the window. This was the first time that she and Landon had eaten out together and no one else was with them. Once again, it brought thoughts of Dallas into the forefront of her mind. She refused to let her thoughts go to the dark side. He would be coming home soon.

She had been surprised when the store had told her they would deliver her furniture the next day. They had everything she had ordered in the storehouse, so she'd of course said yes. The call from them came while she was eating, so she hurried and headed home. She had to get everything ready for tomorrow. She was so glad to be distracted from the emotions she felt about Dallas if she gave in to them.

She had put the baby to bed and then she walked into the living room. She was going to have the movers remove the furniture that was in here and put it out on the porch. She was going to have to figure out what to do with that furniture. But she could imagine this living room actually being hers after she thought about it, and hopefully Dallas would like what she had bought also. There was room for other things in this big room, so he could add to it, or she would get rid of this and they would pick out something together. She was just glad at the moment to be starting her new life here on this ranch with things she had chosen. And hopefully she would get to start her life here on this ranch with the man she had chosen.

She did have a good feeling about it and that was a huge relief.

* * *

Dallas drove toward home. It had been the longest drive and the longest two days there, and now on this fourth day, it was seeming as if it would never end.

He had talked to Lorna on the phone every evening, and she had told him that she had bought new furniture and that it looked great. They had delivered it the second day and had taken out the furniture in the living room. The guys from the ranch had taken the old furniture to a donation place, which made her not feel so bad about removing it from the house. Dallas was excited in those moments to hear her excitement, but he had a distinct feeling she was covering up missing him. He was covering up missing her also.

He had barely been able to make it without seeing her. When he reached the outskirts of Star Gazer Island, he made a quick, direct drive to the ranch. When he parked the truck, instantly the front door opened, and she rushed out. He opened his arms and she flew into them.

He lifted her face and kissed her. "I missed you," he muttered as they kissed.

When they finished kissing, she smiled. "I'm glad you had a good trip. I'm glad you're home."

He did not miss that she had said home and how much it meant to him. "I'm thrilled to be here. Show me what all you've been doing while I was gone."

She grinned at him. "Come on in. And, honestly, if you don't like it, please tell me, because I don't want anything you don't like."

They walked into the living room. It had changed in a great way. Yes, there was beautiful furniture. It was relaxed, with the colors being cream and brown. New end tables, one on each end of the couch, and a great-looking coffee table in front of the couch that was like a big chest, were very nice and continued to bring the atmosphere into relaxation. She had purchased candlesticks for the mantel; there was a painting up there also. It was a view of a beautiful lake. He spotted the name and smiled.

"You got your painting from Nina."

"I did. And I love it. So what do you think about everything else?"

"I think you are a very talented young woman. It looks great."

"Thank you. Things can be added, though. This is a big room."

"Yup. And I'm sure you'll figure out as you go what you want."

She looked a little hesitant and then smiled. "True. One day."

The disappointment couldn't be missed, and he hated putting it there. He suspected she'd wanted him to maybe put in his ideas.

* * *

On Monday, Lorna rode with Dallas out to his family ranch. Nina had called and asked her whether she wanted to come out there with him and maybe help some with what they were decorating. She'd said Lorna was more than welcome to just bring the baby and visit with them. They didn't want her to do something that she couldn't do with the baby, but they didn't want to not invite her if it was something she wanted to do.

Lorna wanted to do it so bad and right now, trying hard to get used to Dallas being back and still not taking their relationship to the next stage by asking her to marry him was confusing. She had instantly agreed and was thrilled to be heading out to the ranch with Dallas. They had had a good week. He had worked on the ranch and started working with the horses, and it was fun. She had spent time out there watching him and hoping so much that he might ask the important question.

Despite still no marry-me question, she was happier than she had been in a long time. Not counting the night she got to hold Landon for the first time. But that had been a very special night—not only was her baby born, but her future love had rescued her. It had been a life-changing night.

"This should be fun. Now, I'll be helping put up a tent and things like that, so you sure you're going to be okay just hanging with the girls?"

She laughed. "Yes, I'm crazy about your mom and the few times I met Nina, she was great to me. And really, I'm loving meeting people. This is my new home where I'm going to raise my sweet son, so I'm thrilled to have wonderful new people to get to know."

"Well then, that sounds great. My mom and Nina both have said very nice things about you, so here we go." He smiled and they drove down the highway.

Soon they pulled into the long drive. She saw the ladies out at the side of the house working on something. As they got closer, she realized they were working on ribbons. When he parked, she got out and got the baby; he went to grab the carrier.

She took Landon. "No, you've got places to go, and me and Landon have places over there. Now go have fun helping. And don't worry about me."

He smiled and, to her absolute joy, he leaned in and kissed her.

"You have fun. Love you."

"I will. You too." Her heart pounded away. She turned and walked toward the ladies.

"Lorna, you're here. We are so excited." Nina put her ribbon down and hurried to give her a quick hug.

Lorna hugged her back.

"I am so thrilled to see you, young woman." Alice hugged her. Then she looked at Landon. "And this baby! Oh, I could look at him every day. Here, let me take him, and Nina can show you around. We've got ribbons to do and then things to get ready so that when the fellas get the tent up and the tables moved in, we'll be ready to get the beginning decoration done." She chuckled and then took the baby, and walked over and sat down. She took Landon out of his carrier and he was smiling as he reached up, trying to touch her.

Nina looked delighted. "Thank you for coming out. I didn't want you to feel left out, and we could also use extra hands. We're getting the basic decoration done today and then over the rest of the week, it will be ready for the different installers to come in and prepare their stuff. Like the light guy will come in tomorrow and hang a bunch of tiny lights all over the ceiling areas."

"That's great. I was so thrilled when I got your call. I'm new in town and this makes me feel like I'm starting to be a part of the town or have friends, you know."

Nina gave her a wink. "Oh, yes, I know. Which is another reason why I thought an invitation would be good."

Nina showed her the size bows she was making, and she jumped in and started to help.

They worked hard on the ribbons. There were about sixty of them. They were going to go on the tables with candle holders and some fresh flowers that were arriving Saturday morning.

Alice had walked the baby and brought him back, sleeping. She put him back in his little carrier. "He went to sleep. Did he need to eat?"

"I had fed him right before we came, so he was full. But he'll be waking up in a little bit and he will be ready."

She chuckled. "Aren't they always? My boys, oh my goodness. My boys ate all the time. It was almost as if I didn't have any in between time. So it's unusual when I see the way most babies are."

Nina laughed. "Well, I can tell you that Jackson is not a normal man—he's just super productive, super kind, and awesome. So all that baby feeding you did with him probably set him up for that. Thank you."

"You're welcome." Alice chuckled. "I'm totally happy to have done it."

"I can tell you that Dallas loves to work," Lorna said. "And he doesn't seem to get tired, so you may have fixed him up with all that breastfeeding you were doing. I hear it works like that too."

Nina and Alice both chuckled.

"Well then, I have to say that as a mom, I did awesome. Success. You're going to do it too," Alice said, then winked.

"Okay," Nina said. "We have to go inside the house, where we are putting together decorations that will go on the dessert tables and the food tables. And by the time we finish that, we'll have a big tent to decorate."

"Sounds great." Lorna reached over and picked up the baby carrier; Nina picked up one of the boxes with the ribbons in it and Alice picked up the other one. They followed Nina into the house. They went through the kitchen, which was beautiful and big, and then they went into the huge dining area. They set the boxes on the dining table, then she pulled out a chair and set the baby carrier in it. The huge table would sit twelve people and if she wasn't mistaken, it would extend out to be able to sit more people. Goodness gracious.

"So did y'all used to, or maybe still do, have huge dinners?" she asked.

Alice chuckled. "When William, my husband, was alive, he ran this business a lot like Jackson does. But in the earlier days, he held a lot of dinners. Back then he knew that whoever wanted to buy his animals enjoyed coming out and having a showing of the animals and then dinner here in the house. Therefore, we held them here often. It was very fun, very busy, and we sold lots of cattle. He had learned that from his own father. But then later, big white tents got popular, like the one going up outside, and they gave us the ability to invite more people to see the cattle and have a huge dinner. This dining room became for family use only."

"Wow, time changes things. But this is beautiful."

"Yes, I think so. I can tell you, I have a vision that one day when all of my sons marry and have children and families that this table will be packed at holidays or special occasions. So I'm very thankful to William for this."

"That is a great story and he sounds like a great man," she said. "Your boys will have a huge family for you, I have a feeling."

Alice grinned. "Sounds perfect."

Nina's dancing eyes met hers. "Well, I'm planning on it and Jackson is too. I just need some other family—you know, sisters-in-law—to help fill this dining room."

Lorna was a bit startled when Nina winked at her and so did Alice. She just looked at them and smiled. "I think that's a great idea too."

CHAPTER TWENTY-ONE

Dallas gazed around. The tent was almost finished and some of the moving team had already started to set up the tables. The ladies could now get in and do their decorating. They were ready.

He and his brothers had been ready to jump in here and help Jackson, to show him they cared and to have fun teasing him some—which they had done. They had been having fun and he was glad because the wedding was going to be a little different; they weren't going to be his best men. It was just going to be Jackson and Nina at the front, and his brothers were going to be on the front row watching them exchange their love vows. Which was fine. He would be sitting beside Lorna.

He was so ready for this same thing; his heart was over the top, it was so ready. And he planned to ask her to marry him after his brother's marriage. He just couldn't bring himself to do it while Jackson was getting married. This was Jackson's and Nina's time, and it was going to be awesome.

"You sure are lost in thought," Jackson said as he came up from where he had just hammered the large attachment into the ground to hold this section of the tent down. It was the last one. The tent was ready.

"Sorry about that."

Jackson studied him. "Why don't you take a walk with me? This is done."

"I don't want to take up your time. This is all about you today."

Jackson laughed. "Then you have to walk with me, because right now the one thing I want to do is talk to you. So, fall in step, brother."

He watched his brother start walking toward the pasture and he joined him. What else could he do?

"Tell me, what's going on between you and Lorna?"

He had known that's what he was going to ask him. "I love her. And I want to ask her to marry me. I want to help her build up her ranch business—that was already a success but can diminish if she doesn't know how to build it. It financially wouldn't matter because she had the money from the invention, but the ranch does well and I want to help build it into a greater success."

"That sounds great."

"Yeah, but mostly I want to be with her and Landon. I still can't believe how I met her or that sweet baby, but that's what I want to do. I want to marry her. I don't need her money or her land. I need her. I was planning on asking her a couple of days after you and Nina have gotten married. There's no way I wanted to do it before y'alls wedding. I didn't want to steal anything from your wedding. And I wanted me asking her to be special."

"Man, I am so excited that you found someone. We've all talked about it, and y'all just seem like a perfect match. And Nina is crazy about her. She thinks you two are absolutely perfect together, as do I—and Mom, too."

"Thank you. I'm thrilled, and I think she's not just perfect for me, but fits in to our family. And I think Dad would have loved her."

Jackson stopped and studied him. His eyes suddenly lit up.

Dallas ducked his chin, studying him with curiosity. "Why are you looking like that?"

"Because I just had a great idea. That I can't mention at the moment. But I will later. Anyway, I think that we should go back and finish out the decorations and get ready for this wedding. And I just need to tell you that I'm thrilled for you. I don't necessarily need you to put off asking her to marry you until I get married. If I were you, I would go for it."

Dallas wanted to. "I'll consider it. Thanks for bringing me out here. Maybe I've been wrong, thinking I need to put it off until after your wedding."

"Maybe. But I would pick a special moment and do it soon. Even tomorrow."

"I've been considering how and where I could ask her, so I won't go up there right now and ask her. I have to have a plan."

Jackson patted him on the shoulder. "You'll figure it out. Now let's get back. Hopefully, you're feeling better?"

"Yes, very much." He was. He just had to decide when now.

* * *

Jackson and Nina waved good-bye at the end of the evening as everyone left.

"They were all so wonderful," Nina said as they went back inside.

"Yes, they were." He took her hand and led her out onto the patio. They sat down in the swing and he put an arm around her. "It was a great day."

"Oh, it was so wonderful. Your family is just awesome, and Lorna is too."

"They are. And they love you. I think Lorna is great and fits in so well. That was really nice of her to come help."

"I thought so too. Do you realize she and Dallas love each other? So very much."

"I do. It's obvious."

"She was helping me, and I had to ask her a few questions—I can't help myself; I just think they're so perfect for each other. She said they were probably getting married, although he hasn't asked her yet."

"He talked to me a little bit today and he hasn't wanted to ask her before we get married. He's trying to hold back until maybe a couple days after the wedding. But I told him to go ahead and ask her."

"I think they should go ahead and get married."

He looked at her, curiosity in his brain because he had the funny feeling that she was thinking the same thing that he had been thinking. The same thing he had planned to ask her. "And what are you thinking?" He grinned.

Her eyes danced. "Well, we're getting married and I love you so much—I do, I do, I do. I was wondering how you would feel—of course, I don't even know if they would agree—but I was wondering how you would feel about them getting married with us? If we get them to get a license by Wednesday, they'd be within the seventy-two hour window and can be in the wedding."

He laughed and pulled her into his arms. "I think that's an absolute awesome thought. And actually, the reason I brought you out here was because I wanted to ask you what you thought about it."

She pushed back and grinned at him. "See there? You and I think a lot alike on a lot of things. So what do we do?"

"I think we need to go out to their ranch in the morning and talk to them. Well, no, we can't do that...he has to ask her to marry him first." He was confused at the moment. "So do I need to go out and see him first and tell him what our plan is? Tell him that if he should ask her to marry him tomorrow and then tell her they are invited to join into our wedding?"

"Yes, I think that's what needs to be done. And tell him that I am totally and completely on board. That, other than marrying you, nothing would please me more than to share our wedding with them."

"I really love you."

She smiled. "And I really love you." And then he kissed her.

* * *

The morning after they had helped decorate for the

wedding, Dallas was surprised to get a call from Jackson, asking him to meet him in town for breakfast. So of course, he headed that way. He explained to Lorna what he was doing and made sure she was okay.

She wished him and Jackson a good breakfast and seemed happy.

He was happy, too, but he was trying to figure out when would be a good time to ask her to marry him. Jackson had encouraged him to go ahead and ask her, and he knew that that would make her happy. He could feel that she was worried about why he hadn't asked her since he'd told her he loved her. He worried now that she might think he wasn't sure yet.

He reached the restaurant and climbed out, and saw Jackson sitting outside at a picnic table in the far area of the outdoor space. He headed that way.

"I am glad you made it." Jackson grinned at him.

"Well, of course I would. I'm curious about what you want to talk about, but I'll meet you for breakfast anytime."

"Good. I already ordered our favorite for us. You know, that breakfast burrito thing they make."

He smiled. "Great. You know I really like that thing."

Jackson studied him. "Oops, here comes our food," he said, and they waited for the waitress to place it on the table, including coffee. After she walked away, he looked at his brother with seriousness. "Me and my sweet fiancée have watched you and Lorna, and we had a meeting together last night. She had talked with Lorna and had gotten the yes that Lorna wanted to marry you but was uncertain if you were ready. Or if you, in the long term, wouldn't choose her."

Dallas dropped his fork and his stomach rocked. "She thinks I might not marry her? I haven't asked her, but I've told her I love her over and over. I just haven't asked her because like I told you, I didn't want to interrupt your wedding. But I didn't know that I was causing her to think maybe I wouldn't. As a matter of fact, this morning when you called, I was trying to decide if I could ask her to marry me tonight."

Jackson grinned. "That's perfect with what I'm going to suggest."

"What are you going to ask me?"

"Nina and I would like for y'all to join us in our wedding Saturday. We'd like it to be a double wedding."

Dallas stared at his brother, completely shocked. "You're serious."

Jackson grinned. "I am, and Nina might be more serious than me. She's crazy about Lorna and she thinks that a double wedding would be perfect. And I do, too. If you do. But you'd have to ask her; then, if she agrees, y'all will go and get your wedding license."

Dallas stared at his brother, his heart pounding out of control. *He wanted this. Was it possible? Would she want it or would it scare her away?*

* * *

The day after helping Nina work on setting up the wedding, Lorna was so happy she'd gotten to help but she was also once again fighting the sadness of Dallas not having asked her to marry him. She was folding baby clothes and that left her brain wide open to try to figure out why. Which she'd done a bunch of times with no success.

Then Dallas came into the laundry room, startling her. He looked good. His hair was combed neatly and not in a cowboy hat; it was in his hands in front of a starched, very nice shirt and starched jeans. Her heart instantly began to pound. *Was he going somewhere?*

He smiled, walked over to her, and took her hand. "Is the baby sleeping?"

"I just put him down." *What was going on?*

"Then can you come with me?" Without waiting, he walked out the laundry room door and toward the doors that led out onto the porch.

She would go anywhere with this man.

When they got outside, he continued to hold her hand and stared out at the ranch. She was so curious.

He turned and looked at her. "I just want to tell you how blessed I am to have found you and your unborn baby that day. I've told you that before, but I never told you how much meeting you changed my life. I knew that I was going to have to leave my rodeo career, but I wasn't exactly ready. And then you needed me on the beach, and then you needed me here on the ranch. And then *I* needed you, because you filled my heart. And you made me know that I wanted more than just getting on a bull every evening and competing for an award. I wanted far more—I wanted you. And your sweet son. And I've been putting this off way too long." Still holding her hand, he went down on his knee and looked up at her.

Oh! Lorna's heart exploded as she realized what he was doing. Tears formed in her eyes and she just blinked and looked into his, waiting for the words she'd been ready for so long.

"Lorna, will you marry me? Will you make my life complete and make me the happiest man in the world?"

Tears rolled freely down her cheeks. "Y-yes. Yes."

He rose and swept her into his arms, spinning them around as he kissed her—even though her face was now covered with tears.

She was actually going to be Mrs. Dallas McIntyre.

After they had kissed, he led her to the porch swing and they sat down. He faced her, still holding her hand. "Here's my next question. Would you marry me Saturday? Jackson and Nina have asked if we would join them at the wedding, and we would all get married at the same time. We still have time if we go tomorrow."

What? She couldn't speak. She stared at him and he nodded, as if knowing she was completely uncertain about what he had said. "I'm confused."

"Here's the story. They just wanted to make sure that if we wanted to get married that we would join them—and believe me, they are excited at the idea that we might want to. I then told him that I had planned on asking you to marry me two days after they were married because I didn't want to interrupt their special wedding time. And then he completely surprised me with his offer. And I personally would love to do it. I wished I had already been married to you for a very long time."

She couldn't believe this. She thought about the dress she had bought to wear to the wedding, a soft cream-toned dress that came ankle high and would actually work as a wedding dress. She smiled at him and gasped. "They are so great. And yes. I want to be your wife, and Saturday is the perfect time to get married."

Life had just turned into a dream.

CHAPTER TWENTY-TWO

On Saturday, the day her son was marrying his future wife, Alice drove to Lorna's home to pick her and the baby up. Today had been a total, but overjoyed day for her when Nina had called and said that they had a surprise. That Dallas was also getting married and could she stop by and pick up Lorna and the baby so that Lorna could get dressed at the ranch with her. She had known how excited this would make Lorna.

When she got there, she looked around to see her son, but she didn't. This was his wedding day, so he probably wasn't even sleeping here. She knew he slept in a different room, but this had been the night leading up to his wedding, so she assumed he hadn't spent the night here. She reached the door and Lorna met her, opening the door before she knocked. They hugged.

"I can't believe I'm getting married today," Lorna said. "I'm so blessed and happy."

"I'm thrilled you are marrying my son today, and this was a brilliant idea by Nina and Jackson. You and Dallas are such a perfect couple and it's great that y'all are getting married. The fact that two sons are getting married at the same moment makes it super special. So are you ready?"

"Yes, I've got my bag packed. The baby is ready, so we can load it all up and hit the road to my dream coming true."

Alice smiled. She loved this young woman. "Let's do it."

Within minutes, they were on their way.

"I hope I can be the kind of wife that he needs."

Alice glanced at her. "You already are. You two are perfect together. So don't be worrying about that. I've never seen him so happy as when he is with you. Oh, he used to be utterly happy when he was riding a bull. But when he's with you, just the few times I've seen you two together, he was another guy. Completely, crazy in love with you and the baby—which makes it even better."

"That's wonderful. And I love him so much."

"And that is the only thing I ask from a daughter-in-law."

She got them to the ranch, and it was easy to see

that last-minute things for the wedding were being done. They got to the door of the kitchen and Nina came in through the living room.

"You made me so happy!" Nina exclaimed. "I am so thrilled to have you and Dallas join me and Jackson. Makes the special wedding even more special."

They hugged and Alice's heart went crazy, she was so thrilled.

They took all the clothing to a guest room, across from the room where there were chairs sitting in front of a large mirror and a local hairstylist, ready and waiting. Nina had thought of everything. They talked about their hopes and dreams as they had their hair put up in beautiful curls—making sure they had different styles. They were getting married at the same time but didn't want the same look.

They had all taken care of the baby and Alice was so thrilled to have her first grandchild. Yes, he wasn't her natural grandson, but she was claiming him all the way and overjoyed to do so.

When they were both busy with the hair, she went out onto the porch with him. It was so beautiful. She looked at her watch, seeing that within an hour people would be arriving and soon her world was going to change. She was now going to have two daughters-in-law and a grandson. And Nina had said she was ready to have a baby, so suddenly Alice was looking at a whole different world than what she'd been looking at just months ago. It was exciting. It was wonderful. She and Seth had committed to a relationship and she was overjoyed. Two of her sons were getting married, and her restaurant and inn was keeping her busy. It was a success and she loved it. It was all amazing.

And then there was Riley. He was about to start a project of his own out by the ocean and she was very intrigued by it. The ranch had enough hired hands that he wasn't tied down to it. She was looking forward to what he did next. She wondered how long it would be before he and Tucker finally found the women of their dreams. But right now, this was about Jackson and Dallas and the women of their dreams. She turned to carry the baby back inside and to make sure she was ready for the wedding.

She was so overjoyed, and them saying "I do" couldn't happen soon enough.

* * *

"Oh guys, y'all look pretty fancy," Riley said as he entered the dressing room where Jackson and Dallas were dressed in their suits.

"You like our suits?" Dallas grinned at his brother. Riley had on a suit, and so did Tucker.

"I like it a lot. Y'all just have this look about you

that says y'all are about to be happy, happy, happy men."

Jackson laughed. "Well, it's true. I thought it was just going to be me happy, happy, happy today, but you can tell Dallas is so excited, he could pass out on us he's so excited."

They all looked at him.

"It's true. I'm so ready I can hardly stand the waiting. In these last few weeks, my life has completely changed. I started out so stinkin' sad and broken-hearted over my injury and then things changed. Now, when can we go out there and make this happen?"

"Well, I was looking out there at the preacher and I heard him tell you to come out and join him when he steps up onto the top step. He's not on it yet. But I'll let you know and you two can have a race to him. Then me and Tucker will go around and escort Mom to her seat. Seth will follow her, carrying the baby. And we'll have a seat beside them." He smiled, then nodded toward the door. "He just stepped up onto the step, so we better all get in place."

Dallas's heart lurched with excitement. Riley and Tucker left, grinning.

Jackson looked at him. "All right, you ready?"

Dallas grinned. "More ready for this than anything I've ever wanted in my entire life. Thank you for asking us to join you and Nina. Now let's both go be happy."

Jackson put a hand on his shoulder and squeezed. "I'm with you, brother. Here we go."

Dallas was overjoyed that this day was here. At last—he was about to be a married man. He was about to be the happiest man alive.

He looked at Jackson as they prepared to walk out and join the pastor. "I won't ever be able to repay you for this opportunity. It's a dream come true."

Jackson met his stare. "Believe me, it's that kind of day for me too. Having you join me makes it even more special."

The preacher looked to the side, at them, and nodded. They looked at each other and grinned, then walked out and took their spot on either side of the preacher. Then they watched the entrance of the beautiful tent, as the audience did too.

The piano played the wedding song and beautiful Nina entered the tent first. She was gorgeous and looked so happy that she radiated. Right behind her, just a few steps, the most wonderful person in the world—the most beautiful and the love of his life, the miracle of his life—Lorna walked in. His heart pounded as he watched her come up the aisle.

Her gaze was locked with his, and he could tell

she was fighting back tears. She was an emotional woman, a special woman.

She paused when Nina reached the preacher. The preacher smiled at Nina. "Nina Hanson, are you here to give yourself to Jackson McIntyre?"

"Yes, more than ready," Nina said, smiling widely.

"Then, Jackson, take her hands."

They locked hands and turned to watch Lorna finish her few steps to the preacher.

"Lorna Jordan, are you ready to marry Dallas McIntyre?"

Lorna looked at him, her eyes full of emotion. "I am, with all of my heart."

He took her hands, feeling blessed more than anybody else in the world, and they turned toward the preacher. The next few moments, as the preacher said the vows to Jackson and Nina and then repeated them to him and Lorna, were the happiest moments of his life. And from Lorna's expression, she felt the same. He knew his brother and new sister-in-law's joy was the same.

His life had been totally confused when he'd found her on the beach. And then, in the most unbelievable way, Lorna had changed his life, and nothing had ever been the same. And thank God; standing here with her hands in his, now as husband

and wife, he knew life would only get better from here on.

"I love you, Lorna McIntyre, with all my heart." He lowered his lips to hers and kissed her.

Jackson did the same, and the crowd clapped and cheered for all of them.

"I love you too," Lorna whispered as the cheers carried on.

"Life is only going to get better from here on in," he repeated his thoughts with a smile as he wrapped her in his arms. And his heart.

* * *

Alice was smiling as she carried her new sleeping grandchild, Landon, up to her new married sons and each of their beautiful brides. "I am so proud of y'all," she said to them.

"I am, too. Congratulations," Seth agreed.

Hugs and smiles went all around; then Dallas took the baby and cuddled him and smiled. "I hate to tell my brother that I'm the happiest man in the world. I've got this gorgeous woman and this adorable baby, and he and his beautiful bride made it possible."

Jackson and Nina both chuckled. Then Jackson placed his hand on Dallas's shoulder. "I hate to disagree with you—you do have a very special bride and baby, and you are a very blessed man. But I have to say that for me, I am the most blessed man in the world, with a wonderful woman as my wife." He hugged Nina, and she kissed him.

Watching her two sons be so happy thrilled Alice. She looked at Seth as he slipped his hand around hers and smiled. Her heart pounded and she knew he, too, was very special. She loved Seth and one day it would be them getting married. He smiled back at her, completely understanding what she was thinking.

Her life and those of her sons and friends were changing, but she knew her past and the love she'd had and lost were what made these moments even more special. Dreams had died; new dreams arose, even if one hadn't expected it to happen. And she knew that William was most likely watching his sons find happiness and was just as happy as she was. And knowing that made her even more happy. Knowing he would be happy for her the day, in the future, when she decided to marry Seth sent an ease through her. One day at a time, though.

One day at a time.

EPILOGUE

Riley stood at the edge of the dance floor, watching his two brothers dance with their brides. He had enjoyed tonight so much. His brothers were so very happy. And he was thrilled for them. And he knew his dad would be.

"They look good and ecstatic. Don't they look happy?" Tucker asked.

"Incredibly. So, are you thinking about looking for love?" He looked at his brother.

Tucker shrugged. "I don't know. I figure if I'm to marry that I'll meet her when I'm supposed to. I don't really go crazy just looking for somebody. How about you?"

"I don't know. I want to get married. And I have to say, I've been impressed by someone, but I just barely met her, so I don't know where she lives. Like you, if it's supposed to happen, it'll happen at the destined time. But I want to open that beach camp and who knows, maybe I'll meet exactly who I want to meet there. But that's what I'm concentrating on when we leave here. No more thinking about it. I want to be happy and that is all I can think about right now. It will make me happy."

Tucker stared at him with his mouth kind of open, and then he smiled. "Well, I think that's awesome. And if you need any help, I can help you. And in all honesty, it also sounds interesting."

"Well, thanks. I'm sure I'll be calling. However, your work on the ranch is far greater than mine, so I wouldn't take advantage of you. I've got to get a whole lot of things lined up before the actual building and preparing begins. It may take until next summer, but next summer that place is going to be ready."

He watched the dancing going on and could imagine a dance going on at his camping grounds. He was ready. He hadn't come up with a name yet, but he would. It was probably going to be something like McIntyre Ranch Camping. He wasn't sure; it might need to be more creative than that, but he would come up with something. He grinned; he hadn't been this excited in forever.

He watched Jackson smiling at Nina, and Dallas kissing Lorna. The two couples looked happier than any of the couples he'd ever seen. Maybe one day he'd find that.

Until then, he was making a campground focusing mainly on single women. Women who got together to enjoy life despite not having a man there to help them. He thought that was pretty cool.

And he was going to give them another place to enjoy here on McIntyre Ranch.

The saying on the side of the trailer of the woman who had unknowingly got him thinking about opening a campground popped into his head. *Live, Laugh, Love and Enjoy Life… It's just too dang short.*

If he thought about his dad, taken at what Riley considered too young, this small camper and the woman driving it, her upbeat mood—he knew he was throwing himself into this project.

And if he was lucky, maybe the camper would come out and he'd get to know her name.

Dear Readers,

Thank you so much for reading! I hope you enjoyed this book and that you'll check out the next book in the *Star Gazer Inn of Corpus Christi Bay* series.

WHAT HOPES ARE MADE OF
Star Gazer Inn of Corpus Christi Bay, Book Three

Catch up as the story continues on Star Gazer Island. Three women find friendship and courage on the shores of Corpus Christi Bay. Come visit the Star Gazer Inn, with a side trip to the McIntyre Ranch, as widow Alice McIntyre finds her way between two worlds.

The Star Gazer Inn is packed as the summer nights cool off, but temperatures are rising as Alice and Seth are exploring a new level of their "friendship" and both are nervous.

Oh the "Glamping" we will do...Riley has more than he bargained for as the venue opens, and the women show up in droves ready to be pampered while roughing it on the ranch's beach side retreat. And the woman he's been hoping he would find just pulled into the park...

Jackson and Nina are expecting...puppies!

And Lisa is not happy when an old flame shows up as a guest at the Inn.

Put your feet up, grab a glass of sweet iced tea, or a glass of your favorite wine and enjoy time on the Texas coast.

More Books by Debra Clopton

Star Gazer Inn of Corpus Christi Bay
What New Beginnings are Made of (Book 1)
What Dreams are Made of (Book 2)
What Hopes are Made of (Book 3)

Sunset Bay Romance
Longing for Forever (Book 1)
Longing for a Hero (Book 2)
Longing for Love (Book 3)
Longing for Ever After (Book 4)
Longing for You (Book 5)
Longing for Us (Book 6)

Texas Brides & Bachelors
Heart of a Cowboy (Book 1)
Trust of a Cowboy (Book 2)
True Love of a Cowboy (Book 3)

New Horizon Ranch Series
Her Texas Cowboy: Cliff (Book 1)
Rescued by Her Cowboy: Rafe (Book 2)
Protected by Her Cowboy: Chase (Book 3)
Loving Her Best Friend Cowboy: Ty (Book 4)
Family for a Cowboy: Dalton (Book 5)
The Mission of Her Cowboy: Treb (Book 6)
Maddie's Secret Baby (Book 7)
This Cowgirl Loves This Cowboy: Austin (Book 8)

Turner Creek Ranch Series
Treasure Me, Cowboy (Book 1)
Rescue Me, Cowboy (Book 2)
Complete Me, Cowboy (Book 3)
Sweet Talk Me, Cowboy (Book 4)

Cowboys of Ransom Creek
Her Cowboy Hero (Book 1)
The Cowboy's Bride for Hire (Book 2)
Cooper: Charmed by the Cowboy (Book 3)
Shane: The Cowboy's Junk-Store Princess (Book 4)
Vance: Her Second-Chance Cowboy (Book 5)
Drake: The Cowboy and Maisy Love (Book 6)
Brice: Not Quite Looking for a Family (Book 7)

Texas Matchmaker Series
Dream With Me, Cowboy (Book 1)
Be My Love, Cowboy (Book 2)
This Heart's Yours, Cowboy (Book 3)
Hold Me, Cowboy (Book 4)
Be Mine, Cowboy (Book 5)
Operation: Married by Christmas (Book 6)
Cherish Me, Cowboy (Book 7)
Surprise Me, Cowboy (Book 8)
Serenade Me, Cowboy (Book 9)
Return To Me, Cowboy (Book 10)
Love Me, Cowboy (Book 11)
Ride With Me, Cowboy (Book 12)
Dance With Me, Cowboy (Book 13)

Windswept Bay Series
From This Moment On (Book 1)
Somewhere With You (Book 2)
With This Kiss (Book 3)
Forever and For Always (Book 4)
Holding Out For Love (Book 5)
With This Ring (Book 6)
With This Promise (Book 7)
With This Pledge (Book 8)
With This Wish (Book 9)
With This Forever (Book 10)
With This Vow (Book 11)

About the Author

Bestselling author Debra Clopton has sold over 2.5 million books. Her book OPERATION: MARRIED BY CHRISTMAS has been optioned for an ABC Family Movie. Debra is known for her contemporary, western romances, Texas cowboys and feisty heroines. Sweet romance and humor are always intertwined to make readers smile. A sixth generation Texan she lives with her husband on a ranch deep in the heart of Texas. She loves being contacted by readers.

Visit Debra's website at www.debraclopton.com

Sign up for Debra's newsletter at
www.debraclopton.com/contest/

Check out her Facebook at
www.facebook.com/debra.clopton.5

Follow her on Twitter at @debraclopton

Contact her at debraclopton@ymail.com

If you enjoyed reading *What Dreams are Made of*, I would appreciate it if you would help others enjoy this book, too.

Recommend it. Please help other readers find this book by recommending it to friends, reader's groups and discussion boards.

Review it. Please tell other readers why you liked this book by reviewing it on the retail site you purchased it from or Goodreads. If you do write a review, please send an email to debraclopton@ymail.com so I can thank you with a personal email. Or visit me at: www.debraclopton.com.

Printed in Great Britain
by Amazon